SECTOR 64: FIRST CONTACT

A SECTOR 64 PREQUEL NOVELLA

DEAN M. COLE

CANDTOR PRESS

Sector 64: First Contact

Published by CANDTOR PRESS

Dean@DeanMCole.com

Also by Dean M. Cole

Get *Solitude: Dimension Space Book One* Today!
(Read the *Solitude* sneak peak at the end of this book.)

The Martian meets *Gravity* when Earth's last man, Army Captain Vaughn Singleton, discovers that the last woman is stranded alone aboard the International Space Station. Commander Angela Brown could reverse the event that swept humanity from Earth's surface ... if only she could get there. If you like action-packed, page-turning novels, you'll love the electrifying action in this award-winning, apocalyptic thriller.

The Complete *Sector 64* Set

The *Sector 64* Timeline

1947 - *First Contact* a *Sector 64* Prequel Novella
Today - *Ambush* - Book One of the *Sector 64* Duology
Tomorrow - *Retribution* - Book Two of the *Sector 64* Duology

(Read the sneak peak of *Ambush* at the end of this book.)

FIRST CONTACT

"I'm not at liberty to discuss the government's knowledge of extraterrestrial UFOs at this time. I am still personally being briefed on the subject."

— Richard Nixon

CHAPTER 1

Under a dark moonless sky, Major Anthony Spinelli gazed east from the cockpit of his P-51 Mustang.

Staring down the long runway, he nodded. "Good a time as any." Then Tony sighed and squeezed the radio transmit trigger.

"Roswell Army Air Field Tower, this is Black Crow Three. Ready for departure."

"Roger, Black Crow Three." The Army air traffic controller paused, his mic still active. Finally, he said, "Are you sure you're ready, sir?"

Tony knew the sergeant and knew that his question had nothing to do with the readiness of his fighter aircraft.

"I'm fine, Rob." After a pause of his own, Tony sighed and keyed the radio. "Now if you don't mind, got an appointment with this morning's sunrise. The squadron commander wants a couple of hours on this ole Stang, make sure the mechanics got it right this time."

"Okay, sir ... Listen, I'm sorry for your loss—"

"Dammit, Sergeant Johnson. How about you just clear me for takeoff?"

Shocked silence streamed from the radio. Finally, the controller's voice returned, tight and curt. "Sorry, Major ... Black Crow Three cleared for departure, Runway Zero-Eight."

Tony winced, but he bit back an apology. After a brief hesitation, he shook his head and dutifully repeated the takeoff clearance. Then he applied full throttle. The Mustang's 1500-horsepower engine roared, and its eleven-foot-wide prop quickly screwed the ten thousand-pound plane into the air.

Tony patted the throttle. "Purring like a kitten."

Of course, it had always run smoothly at first. The glitch only manifested after a few minutes of flight, although Tony believed they had finally found the culprit. He expected an uneventful flight this morning.

A quarter-hour later, as he guided the plane up to twenty thousand feet, Tony patted the throttle again. "Good to go."

None of the earlier issues had returned. Regardless, the squadron commander wanted him to make doubly sure that it didn't. The Old Man had instructed him to fly it for two hours minimum. Tony thought the commander likely saw this as a test flight for him as much as for the Mustang.

He turned the fighter to a heading that would take him to a site only seventy-five miles to the west. Not far, but better than flying in big circles. The destination was Trinity, the location of the first nuclear bomb detonation. Tony shook his head. He couldn't believe that only two years had passed since that first nuclear test in 1945. The entire world had changed in those 24 months. A world war had ended, and a cold one had replaced it, but none of that mattered now, not after what had happened to his family.

The lights of Roswell Army Air Field disappeared behind him. Tony looked overhead. High clouds obscured even the stars from view. In the dark, moonless night, he couldn't see a thing through the fighter's canopy. Absolute blackness filled it as if the entire universe had disappeared, leaving Tony and his airplane in a black void that matched his mood.

As the powerful engine droned, Tony thought back on his numerous flights over World War II Germany. The plane's familiar reverberation had accompanied him through dark days and darker nights, through life and death. And he'd done it all willingly enough.

He'd done it to keep the war 'over there.' He'd done it for them, to keep them safe.

And now...

For long minutes, Tony stared into the blackness that had swallowed his aircraft. He shook his head and swallowed back the lump that was trying to choke him.

As good a day as any? What had he meant by that?

The scary thing was, Tony didn't really know.

Some minutes and several miles later, he realized he was staring at a point of white light. His hungry eyes had latched onto it of their own accord. It looked as if an improperly shielded bulb in the cockpit was reflecting off of the inside of his canopy. He searched for the source but soon realized it was indeed coming from outside, in the sky ahead of his airplane. The white pinpoint of light appeared to hover ahead of the Mustang. A quick check of its navigation instruments revealed he had only covered half the distance to the Trinity site. Sierra Blanca's 12,000-foot peak still lay somewhere ahead, but the light was at his current altitude: 20,000 feet, well above the mountain.

Tony tried to blink the point into focus, but it refused to resolve.

"Is that another airplane?"

His hand tensed on the control stick. A stationary light meant that the two aircraft had to be closing head-on, flying right at one another!

He banked the Mustang hard right. When he leveled off again, the light of the other aircraft began to slide off the left side of the fighter's canopy. The two airplanes were no longer on a collision course. The other plane would pass just off his left wing.

As it neared, the other aircraft's light grew wider and appeared to shift its spectrum, blossoming into a multicolored ring. Tony blinked furiously, trying to resolve its source. Instead of the expected slim profile of an airplane, he glimpsed a squat, symmetrical form. The colorful band of light seemed to straddle its center horizontally.

Suddenly, the shape and its girdling ring of light darted lightning-fast.

Tony flinched, jerking the stick to avoid the plane, but before the

Mustang could respond, the odd-shaped craft had jogged across the nose of the rocking Stang and stopped a half mile off Tony's right wing. The entire maneuver had taken a fraction of a second.

"What the hell?!"

Tony flinched again as the thing darted past his right side and then disappeared behind him, blazing east and passing out of sight almost too quickly to register. One moment, it had been there, hanging off to Tony's right, the next it was gone, leaving only a ghostly streak burned across his night-adapted retinas.

He looked over his right shoulder and shook his head.

Breathing heavily, he said, "What was—?"

Suddenly, blinding light filled his cockpit. Tony's head snapped forward. Dazzled eyes blinked. Then the light returned, and he saw the source. Glowing with the internal brilliance of another lightning bolt, a tremendous thunderstorm filled the front half of his universe.

"Oh, shit!"

The Mustang slammed into the center of the boiling cloud. Wind shear rocked the plane left and right. Tony fought to keep it upright. He tried to turn the fighter around, to guide it east, back out of the thunderstorm, but tremendous blasts of turbulence tossed the plane left, right, and inverted, threatening to snap Tony's tenuous thread of control and throw the fighter from the sky.

With white-knuckled death grips, Tony cycled the throttle, stick, and rudder, fighting to keep the Mustang under control.

Through gnashed teeth, he growled, "Come on, girl!"

Then lightning bolts started firing off in rapid succession. In the span of a few seconds, two of them struck his airplane. The storm had held its pent-up energy until the last minute, hiding its existence, but now it seemed determined to release all of it as rapidly as possible.

Between flashes, Tony felt the entire airframe shudder as a loud report came from his right wing.

Something had hit the plane!

Then another booming impact shook the fighter. Still struggling to keep the Mustang under control, Tony glanced up to see a crack in the canopy.

His eyes widened. "Hail!"

Suddenly, the frequency of the reports increased exponentially, as if a hundred men with sledgehammers had taken to pounding the aluminum-skinned fighter into oblivion.

Another bolt of lightning struck. A spider's web of St. Elmo's fire danced across the skin of the airplane. In the momentary illumination, Tony glimpsed baseball-sized hailstones shattering as they slammed into already ruined wings.

He shook his head. "No, no, no!"

A quick check of his instruments showed that he was losing altitude and airspeed. The increased drag and reduced lift generated by the damaged airfoils and propeller were already pulling the fighter out of the sky.

Tony decided he knew what his earlier statement had *not* meant: it was *not* as good a time as any, not to die anyway. In spite of all that had happened, he wasn't ready to cash it in.

Tony increased throttle to compensate for the decreased lift. In spite of the storm's buffeting, he managed to arrest the plane's descent and stabilize its airspeed, but then another barrage of icy boulders struck. A new crack ran across his canopy.

Now even full throttle wouldn't keep the plane aloft!

"I'm losing her!"

The Mustang was hanging from its prop. The wings would soon stall if—

Then they did!

The fighter snap-rolled, flipping upside down.

"Shit!"

The sharp stall coupled with the torque of a firewalled engine violently tossed the airplane into an inverted flat spin. Rotational G-forces pinned Tony to his seat. He tried to reach for the throttle, but his arm felt as if it weighed a ton. The combination of being inverted and spinning at an insane rate pushed too much blood into his brain, instantly generating an excruciating headache.

Tony grunted with the effort to reach for the throttle.

His eyes widened as he saw the altimeter. Spinning like an

unwinding clock, it plummeted through 5000 feet above sea level. That left less than 2000 feet before he'd hit the area's high desert.

He screamed and with a mighty effort drove his hand forward and finally grabbed the throttle. He pulled it aft, and everything slowed. The sudden drop in rotational G-forces made it feel as if he'd become weightless.

His checklist booklet lazily flapped across the cockpit like a seagull flying in slow motion.

He *was* weightless!

Suddenly, his cockpit lighting dimmed and then faded to black.

The thunderstorm birthed another lightning bolt. Looking into the storm, Tony watched the bolt's energetic fingers slowly arc across the sky.

Then he froze.

The glowing clouds outlined a dark void: a large object hovering just outside his canopy. Tony stared at it in open-mouthed amazement.

The forgotten, fast-moving aircraft had returned, but now it hung motionlessly only a few feet from his head!

The lightning faded, but the multicolored lights he'd seen earlier suddenly filled the air around his fighter. The feathery, ethereal beams shone from no fixtures. It looked as if the air around the craft was glowing.

Tony tore his eyes from the image and checked his altimeter. His fall had stopped. The Mustang's altitude now held stable at 4800 feet. But that was only 1800 above the ground! In the haunting light, he could see his destroyed wings.

Whatever the hell this ... this thing was doing, if it stopped doing it, he'd smack into the ground within a few short seconds.

He had to get out now!

Tony grabbed the canopy and unlatched it. In spite of the damage, it slid back easily. Outside, undulating but otherwise stationary raindrops hung suspended around the pair of vessels.

He stared at the fat-bodied craft. "What are you?!"

Tony looked from the dark silhouette and its rotating ring of multicolored light to his altitude. His stomach said that he was falling, but somehow the altimeter remained unchanged.

He shook his head. "Time to bail!"

Tony unbuckled his harness. His weightless body drifted out of the seat.

Then he closed his eyes as a brilliant lightning bolt struck his fighter again.

At the same moment, a rainbow of colors flooded through his lids. Through slitted eyes, Tony watched the craft's ring of multicolored lights flare and then die.

Then the dark object tumbled away! Just before the thing faded into the storm, another flash of lightning revealed it as a fat saucer shape, like two bowls joined lip to lip.

Suddenly, the storm's wind returned with a vengeance. The suspended raindrops swirled away, and Tony fell out of the still inverted fighter as it violently spun out of sight.

Plummeting toward the waiting desert, Tony frantically yanked at his parachute's ripcord. The pilot chute shot out, dragging its cache of silk from the pack. It unfurled, and the risers snapped taut, jerking him skyward as the parachute arrested his renewed fall.

Tony looked overhead, gazing into the beautiful sight of a fully inflated canopy. "Oh, thank God!"

Then he felt a tremendous updraft pull him higher. His ears popped as the vertical winds drew him deeper into the storm.

He looked up with wide eyes. "No, no, no!"

Last year, an Army Air Corps pilot had bailed in the middle of a thunderstorm and died of exposure and oxygen starvation. The crash investigation team had determined that the man and his parachute had been sucked up into the storm and that its massive updrafts had held him above 45,000 feet for several minutes—more than long enough to induce death from asphyxiation. It was the same lifting mechanism that formed hailstones.

With both hands, Tony pulled down the right riser and grabbed several of the cords, desperately trying to partially collapse the chute, but another surge of rising air yanked the strands out of his hand.

As the winds pulled him higher, a layer of ice began to form on his goggles. The massive storm was doing its utmost to turn him into a human hailstone.

Then, panting and freezing, Tony felt consciousness slipping away.

"No! ... No ..."

CHAPTER 2

Tony woke with a start. A distant brown surface hung beneath his feet. Blinking, he tried to bring it into focus.

A violent shiver racked his soaked body.

Then the world resolved.

"What the hell?!"

Tony flinched. The spasm sent his dangling legs into an arcing swing.

New Mexico's high desert hung a couple of miles beneath the soles of his boots.

Wide-eyed, he looked up. An olive drab parachute towered overhead.

Suddenly, orange light blossomed to his right. Tony's head snapped in that direction. He watched the sun creep above the eastern horizon.

He'd been flying, but ... what?

"My plane!"

"The storm!"

Tony flinched again as a brilliant flash and a tremendous explosion came from his left. He looked that way and saw a towering thunderstorm filling the western sky.

Then his eyes widened as he remembered being in that storm.

"I'm alive!"

When Tony had felt consciousness slipping away, he had thought he was done for. The storm had held him in it long enough for the sun to rise. He must have ridden updrafts and downdrafts for more than half an hour. Fortunately, the storm had spat him out before holding him aloft long enough to kill him. Aside from a splitting headache and a serious case of the shivers, Tony felt alright.

Then the last detail returned.

"That ... thing. What the hell was it?" Tony paused and looked around. "And where in the hell did it go?"

Then he realized he had more immediate issues. He was descending toward one of the region's flat-topped hills, a mesa. He'd be lucky not to tumble off the cliff at its edge. Even if he managed to stick the landing, he'd likely roll onto a damned cactus.

Orange sunlight glinted off of something atop the mesa. Then Tony saw the light reflecting off of hundreds of shiny objects.

"The Mustang?"

He shook his head. No, that can't be from his plane, the pieces were flapping in the breeze. They looked more like foil than the sheet metal skin of an airplane.

Then he saw skid marks scrawled across the hill. Tony followed the lines visually. They ran off the top of the mesa and picked up again about a half mile west, ending at the base of the next hill.

Tony froze, staring open-mouthed at the craft that sat at the end of those scars.

"Son of a bitch ..." he whispered.

That wasn't his plane. It was the fat saucer he'd encountered in the storm.

The thing had crashed!

The sight of the ground rushing up toward Tony's feet snapped him out of his trance. Fortunately, the chute was turned into the wind, so he landed with little lateral drift. He tumbled awkwardly. The rolling impact knocked the breath out of him. As he struggled to draw air, he managed to collapse the chute before it could drag him through a cactus. A moment later, the wheezing man rolled up the chute and pinned it down with his removed harness and a small boulder.

Standing, Tony surveyed his surroundings. He walked over to one of the pieces of foil and picked it up. The small, jagged sheet seemed too light. He could barely feel it. The metallic material rested on his palm like a feather.

Tony flipped it over. The other side of the foil looked black. He held it up. He could see a reflection of the surrounding desert and the sun on its dark surface, but the image looked like a photo negative. Instead of a bright orange orb, the sun looked like a black spot in the center of the image.

Shaking his head, Tony whispered, "How can that be?"

He looked around. Thousands of pieces of the stuff cluttered the ground.

Tony wadded up the foil fragment and dropped it. Before it had fallen an inch from his hand, the piece unfurled and then floated down, zigzagging like a falling feather. Tony picked up another piece and did the same thing, crumpling the sheet until it was a small clump in his fist. Then he opened his hand and the wad unfurled like a flower blooming in fast motion. In less than a second, it flattened out, leaving no wrinkles.

"Jeez!"

He tried it with a few more pieces, always with the same result. Then he saw a crushed cactus. Beyond it, a deep gouge in the sand pointed toward the hilltop's western precipice.

Tony dropped the jagged piece of foil and trotted toward the edge.

The wide draw between the hills scrolled into view. He slid to a stop at the edge of the cliff.

Heart pounding, breathing heavily, Tony stood on the precipice, staring at the black disc wedged into the nape of the next mesa.

"Holy shit ..."

He shook his head.

"What are you?"

Tony finally stopped shivering.

"Good thing it's July," he muttered between breaths.

The desert's dry air had already sucked most of the moisture from his flight suit and leather jacket, and the trek down the mesa's steep slope had warmed him.

Tony stepped over another piece of debris and then did a double take. Something that looked like a portion of a structural member protruded from beneath a foil fragment. He picked up the piece. The small I-beam was about a foot long and an inch wide. The thing was so light it felt as if it might float out of his hand. Tony thought it must be some kind of foam insulation, but when he tried to bend it, the beam wouldn't give. It felt like solid steel cast from thin air.

He tossed it up, and it floated back toward his hand with the celerity of a falling balloon. As the piece slowly somersaulted, Tony glimpsed writing on its side. When it finally landed on his palm, he held the white piece up so that shadows outlined the embossed figures. They looked like a mix of Egyptian hieroglyphs and Asian characters.

"Oh, shit! Russians?"

Then Tony looked closer and shook his head. The Russians used some weird letters, but he didn't recall them looking this odd.

But...

He looked uneasily from the piece to the large disc lying ahead at the base of the hill.

"What the hell are you?" he asked again.

Tony gave the small I-beam another look and then stuffed it into a leg pocket. He continued walking toward the crashed ship.

He wondered if this might be the craft the United Airlines crew had spotted a few days ago.

"A flying saucer?" Tony said, trying out the words.

He'd been thinking it ever since he'd first glimpsed the craft's shape, but spoken aloud, the words sounded ludicrous.

But there one was, a flying saucer right in front of him!

Tony ignored the rest of the debris. Jogging again, he zigzagged between cactuses and crumpled chunks of wreckage. None of it looked like it had come from his Mustang. The airplane was nowhere to be seen. It must've crashed farther west, likely under the now dissipating thunderstorm.

As Tony approached within a hundred yards of the crashed ship, the early morning sun rose from behind the eastern mesa to his rear. He felt its warmth on his back. His shadow stretched toward the strange black object. While the cliff wall behind the saucer glowed in the sun's orange radiance, the dark skin of the disc soaked up the light, just like the foil pieces had.

Tony slowed to a hesitant walk, studying the saucer through slitted eyes. It looked as if the crash had sheared off a significant chunk of its bottom, leaving a large hole. He stopped twenty yards from the disc, reluctant to step any closer.

Tony craned his neck, trying to peer through the hole in the ship. However, the shiny inner surface of the upturned skin that ringed the edge of the gaping maw glistened with the reflected yellow fire of the rising sun. Squinting against its blinding glare, Tony couldn't make out the ship's dark interior.

Stepping hesitantly, he eased closer, a hand held up to shield his eyes from the reflected sunrise. The odor of burned insulation or wiring filled the air, although he didn't see any smoke.

As he stepped within a few feet of the opening, he finally glimpsed something through the hull breach. Tony froze, and his eyes widened as faint gray lines resolved as a complex web that seemed to fill the ship's interior.

"Holy mackerel!" he said through a constricting throat. "Looks like a damned spider's web!"

As if responding to the sound of his voice, the interior of the saucer lit up.

Then Tony saw it.

A silvery being sat suspended at the center of the web!

Suddenly, it began to descend!

"Oh, shit!"

Tony snapped out of his trance and backed away.

He had no interest in being breakfast for some alien spider.

Huh-uh! No way!

He tripped over something and fell hard on his ass.

Two of the spider's silvery legs slid into view.

Tony scurried backward like a fleeing crab. Then he stopped and tilted his head.

"What the hell?"

The body, arms, and head of an ordinary human followed the silver-clad legs. Emerging from the hole in the ship, the limp figure crumpled onto the floor of the desert.

Tony stood and hesitantly walked toward the apparently unconscious … woman? Yeah, a woman. The webbing had deposited her on the sand just outside of the ship's breached hull. Red blood trickled from the corner of her mouth and one of her ears.

As Tony closed to within five feet, the woman's eyes opened. She looked confused.

He stopped. After a moment, Tony found his voice. "What are you? Russian?"

The woman said something in a language that he didn't recognize. Then she swiped a silvery sleeve across the blood on her chin. The skintight metallic material didn't look absorbent, but it soaked up all of the blood, leaving no trace of the red liquid. Then, before his eyes, the stain disappeared from the sleeve as well.

Tony blinked. Speaking louder, he asked, "Are you okay?"

The look of confusion fell from the woman's face. Her eyes widened, and then she spoke again. This time her words sounded more assertive.

Tony still didn't recognize the language, but he was pretty sure it wasn't Russian.

The webbing detached from her and began to retract into the ship. Then her silver suit started flickering.

Tony's eyes widened. "What the …?"

Suddenly, her suit changed shape and color. Now it looked identical to Tony's flight suit and leather jacket.

"How the hell did you do that?!" Tony blurted as he stepped backward again.

The woman didn't answer. She looked at a torn strand of silver webbing that protruded from the black leather elbow of her new jacket. She pulled the web off and wadded it up and then held the clump in an open palm, showing it to Tony.

Had he imagined the silver suit? Had it been an illusion generated by the contrasting light and a panicked mind?

He stopped backing away. Then the strand moved. Transfixed, Tony stared at it, watching the metallic webbing dissolve in her hand like lead melting in a pot. He saw his startled expression reflected in the mirrored surface of the mercurial material.

Shocked into silence, he looked from the woman's palm to the name tag on her flight jacket. He tried to read her name but couldn't make out the letters. They looked ... wrong but somehow familiar.

Tony shook his head. "Who are you?"

The stranger said something as she stepped closer.

Tilting his head, Tony tried to read the odd-looking letters on the tag. Then he recognized them. He'd seen those characters almost every morning of his military career.

It was a mirror image of his own name tag. The backward letters ran from right to left, spelling out Spinelli in reverse.

Tony's eyes widened. "You're a copy!"

He started to step back, but the woman's hand shot out lightning quick and slapped the mercurial goo onto the nape of Tony's neck, behind his left ear.

Fiery pain erupted at the base of his skull. As he stumbled backward, Tony swiped at the silvery mass, but it had turned hard and unyielding. He tripped over something and fell on his ass again. He swiped at the blob a second time, but it had shrunk in size. Using the tips of his fingers, Tony dug, desperately trying to gain purchase, trying to wedge them under an edge of the shrinking mass.

Then it was gone!

The strange woman now stood over Tony, looking down on him with an odd expression. It almost looked like sympathy.

Tony suddenly felt consciousness slipping away.

"What did you do to me? What did you ...?"

Then the dark took him.

CHAPTER 3

Tony opened his eyes and blinked against the harsh blue light that filled his vision. His head felt as if it would split. Squinting, he tried to find something to focus on.

A firm surface supported his prone body. Rolling his head right, Tony saw that he was lying on his back on a tilted floor. About twenty feet away, the gray deck merged with a curved, glowing wall. About ten feet above that point, it joined a ceiling that also glowed with the same blue light.

His headache eased a notch, and the brilliance of the walls and ceiling no longer seemed quite as harsh. He looked left and saw a thick column running floor to ceiling in the center of the room that he now realized was circular.

Tony tried to look toward his feet, but the back of his head stuck to the floor as if he had laid it on a large wad of chewing gum. It gave enough that he saw raw daylight shining through a hole in the wall about twenty feet away.

He was in the ship!

Tony tried to sit, to bolt upright and run for it, but the gum beneath his head pulled him back down. He tried to raise his arms and discovered they were stuck as well.

"Let me go!"

"Cannot."

Tony froze. It hadn't been the word 'cannot,' more like hearing the meaning behind it. But even more disturbing, he hadn't actually heard it at all. The word's intention had echoed in his head, not off of the glowing walls.

He broke from his trance and fought mightily with his restraints.

"Let me go, goddammit!"

"Cannot," the maddeningly calm non-voice repeated.

Tony stopped struggling. He tried to look around the room, seeking the source, but this time the gum held fast. He couldn't move his head. Then the woman in the Air Force uniform with its backward name tag stood from behind him. She had been squatting above him on the tilted floor.

Looking up, Tony regarded her through furrowed eyebrows.

"Let me go!"

She shook her head. Her lips didn't move, but the thought rang out clearly: "Cannot."

"Why the hell not?"

A barely perceptible smile curled the corners of her closed lips. The non-voice and its intentions returned, but her mouth didn't move. "Good. You understand."

Tony only understood one thing. This woman wasn't Russian. Hell, she probably wasn't even from Earth.

"You are correct. Not from your world."

Tony blinked in surprise. "What? I didn't say anything."

"Thoughts I hear, as do you."

Tony felt his heart racing. He fought against the bindings but couldn't break free.

He screamed with frustration. Through a growl, he yelled, "Let me go!"

The woman's Mona Lisa smile faded. Now she looked sorrowful. "Cannot."

Tony felt a twinge at the back of his neck, just below the base of the skull. Then he remembered the gray goo, the pain and losing consciousness. His eyes widened. *What did she do to me?*

"Sorry. We usually sedate for that."

"For what? What did you do?"

"Machines. Tiny. In brain."

"What?! You put a machine in my head?" Tony felt his heart rate redouble, as did his breathing.

She shook her head. "Machines. Not one, millions."

Seeing Tony's widening eyes, the woman held up a hand.

"Calm. No hurt. Machines tiny, like virus but good. Facilitate communication." Her Mona Lisa smile returned. "Facilitate understanding."

Suddenly, Tony felt his blood pressure dropping. His need for air reduced as well.

Her smile broadened, and she nodded. "Machines facilitate calm."

Tony wanted to scream, wanted to yell at the woman, but he could no longer muster the energy or the anger.

"What are you doing to me?" he said in words that seemed to lose import mid-sentence.

The woman didn't answer. She just stared at Tony expectantly.

Unbidden, a stream of images, thoughts, and emotions flowed through his mind. Each elicited the associated word, heard but not spoken aloud. They ran through his mind like cars of a freight train driven through an intersection at top speed. In spite of the calming effect apparently imparted by the little viral machines, Tony's hands clenched into fists, and he ground his teeth together. The sensations threatened to overwhelm him.

Then the stream disappeared, leaving Tony in a welcome sensory void.

"What was that?"

The woman stepped up to Tony's side and dropped to a knee. She cocked her head.

"The machines learned your language," she said, speaking audibly for the first time. She had a strange accent. "Now they teach me ..." She paused and cocked her head sideways. "English?"

The odd accent sounded like that of a South African Army captain whom Tony had served with in the war, but the woman's speech sounded mechanical, her sing-song cadence emphasizing the wrong parts of the sentence.

Tony tried to shake his head. He had to quit thinking of this thing as a woman. It was alien. He now knew he hadn't imagined the silver suit. For all he knew, the alien could change its skin as easily as it had its clothes.

Longingly, Tony gazed down his nose at the hole in the ship. He struggled against the bindings.

Relenting, he pulled his eyes away from the sight of the opening and the beckoning desert beyond. He looked back up to the being.

The alien suddenly looked sad.

"Who are you?" Tony said. "What are you?" He struggled against the bindings. The gum attached to the back of his head constricted, drawing him tight to the floor. Looking through his eyebrows again, he glared at the being. "Why are you here?"

Frowning, she ... No, *it* looked across the interior of the ship, appearing to consider his questions for a long moment. Then it nodded and looked at him intently.

The mental image of a nuclear mushroom cloud blossomed in his mind's eye. It came to him as had the previous impressions but with a visual component this time. He realized that the machines had birthed the vision. Then the image faded, and the being's face again filled his field of view.

Tony blinked. His suddenly dry mouth fell open. "Oh my God! You're here to invade! You're going to nuke us!"

A confused look crossed her ... the being's face. Then its eyes cleared, and its head shook. "No. That was you. You ... exploded ..." It paused again, searching for the word.

Tony felt the machines probe his mind again. Then the alien nodded.

"You exploded atomic weapon." It pointed west. "Near here."

Tony nodded. "Yes, the Trinity test. But that was two years ago."

It nodded again. "Our sensor far away. Light and nuclear signal take two of your years to cross distance."

"Sensor?" His eyes widened. "You had something in space ... watching us? Something two light years away?"

The being shook its head. "Not watching you. We not know you. Millions of sensors across ..."

Tony felt the questing machines again.

It nodded. "Across the galaxy ... the Milky Way. The sensors wait, listen for intelligent life."

He considered her words. They came because they detected our nuclear tests? Shouldn't they have detected our radio waves long before that?

Apparently, the machines in his brain transmitted his thoughts because the being shook its head and raised an eyebrow in a very human-like manner, giving Tony a meaningful look. "Sensors only report life capable of creating trouble." It paused and then pointed east. "Much trouble there."

After a moment, Tony realized the alien was talking about Roswell. That made sense. As far as he knew, the 509th Bomber Group at Roswell Army Air Field had the world's only nuclear-armed airplanes. He tried to quell the thought as soon as it entered his mind, but a nod of the being's head told him that it or its damned machines had read his thoughts.

He tried to shake his head, but the floor held him tight. "So popping nukes means we might be troublemakers? You here to knock us down?"

The being looked confused again, then its head shook. "No. We are here to provide guidance, to ... integrate you into galactic ..."

Tony felt another questioning probe and suddenly understood the meaning behind the being's thought. His eyes widened and, not waiting for the translation, he spoke the word aloud. "Society? You're here to integrate us into galactic society?"

She, it, whatever, gave her beatific smile and nodded.

Struggling against the restraining gum that held his head to the floor, Tony shook his head vigorously. "That's a load of bullshit!"

CHAPTER 4

Tony felt the machines trying to assert calm. He stopped struggling with the restraints and looked at the being through narrowed eyes. "You're here to ... *help* us?" he said dubiously.

"Yes. We do this many, many times."

"Many times ...?" Tony paused, blinking in surprise as the meaning of the words sank in. "How many alien ..." He searched for the right word. "Species? How many alien species are there?"

The being cocked an eyebrow again. "Thousands in the Milky Way."

"Holy moley!" Tony whispered, momentarily forgetting his doubt. "Thousands?"

The being nodded, but then a shadow crossed its face. "But this time is ... different." Its eyes cleared, and the alien again looked at Tony intently. "I need your help."

"What could you need from *me*?"

The being looked around the ship. Then it looked down, back at Tony. "My ship has no ... power. I need ... electricity for my ..." It paused, searching for the right word. Then its eyes widened, and it smiled. "Radio! I need electricity for my radio!"

Tony shook his head vigorously. "Hell no! I'm not helping you call your mothership." He looked around the room. "I was born at night, but not last night, lady. I saw the way your clothes changed. For all I know, your skin changed, too." With his eyes, he gestured toward her leather jacket. "You're probably not a lady at all, might be a lizard under all that. I get you a radio, and you'll call down General Zahn."

The being shook its head. "Machines say you have same ... molecules."

"Molecules?"

The alien nodded. "The same molecules in your cells."

"What are you talking about?"

Suddenly, Tony saw a vision of a coil. It looked like an automobile spring but two of them interwoven with spokes between.

Tony shook his head. "What are those? Coils? What are they supposed to be?"

The image zoomed out, and he saw the coils formed a very tiny portion of a larger, recognizable structure.

Staring at the X and Y, Tony nodded. "Chromosomes."

The image faded, and he saw the alien nodding. "Yes. Molecules form your ... coils, and the coils form chromosomes, as you say."

Tony shook his head. "Your tiny machines could have told you all of that."

The being looked perplexed for a moment. Then it nodded.

Suddenly, a three-dimensional image coalesced in Tony's vision. Unlike the previous images, this one didn't block out everything else. It seemed to float in the air above him, filling much of the ship's interior. It was beautiful. Millions of points of lights swirled in a formation that Tony recognized.

"The Milky Way," he whispered.

He raised a suddenly free hand and tried to touch the swirling lights, but his fingers passed through the image without effect, and the tiny pinpoints of light didn't illuminate his skin.

"How am I seeing this?" he said as he continued to wave his hand through the modeled stars without causing any changes.

The being nodded. "Tiny machines create them. You see it in your mind. Not out here. Virtual, not real."

The thought of the machines altering his brain, altering his *perceptions*, kicked Tony's heart rate into overdrive, but then the sense of calm washed over him again.

"Virtual vision?" he said sedately.

Like cuts in a pie, blue lines appeared at the center of the image and then spread radially from the galactic core to its outer edge. Then a series of concentric rings appeared, first a small one around the center of the galaxy, and then more rings formed outside of it. Finally, the outer one circled the entire galaxy, making it look like a giant dartboard. Adding weight to the analogy, a unique number appeared over each galactic segment.

The being must have been sharing the vision. It pointed into the modeled galaxy and touched the section labeled number one. It was about a third of the way out from the center.

"Sector One," it said. "Argonia." Then it removed its hand from the star field and touched its upper chest. "Argonian."

Then it touched a label about two-thirds of the way out from the galactic center. It had the number sixty-four floating on its surface.

"Sector Sixty-Four. Earth."

Tony reached tentatively for the indicated area. He touched it with one finger. "Earth." Then he touched his own chest. "Earthling. Human."

The woman shook her head. "No. Argonian."

"No," Tony said. "You are Argonian. I am human."

The alien smiled and shook its head again. "We are both Argonian. Same cellular molecules. This is why the tiny machines easily integrate with your brain. Not new to them."

Tony stared back at the alien wordlessly. How could he believe anything it was telling him? A reptilian monster might lie beneath that façade.

The being pointed at Tony again. "Humans may be lost Argonians. Lost long ago." It paused, appearing to seek the right words. Then it nodded. "Tens of thousands of years ago, several colonies lost to space."

Tony shook his head. "Why would I trust you? How do I know you are what you say?"

The alien pointed to Tony's chest. "You have family, yes?"

His eyes narrowed. "Don't talk about my family."

Confusion clouded the being's face. Then its eyes softened. "I have family."

Tony opened his mouth to ask why that mattered, but then a new image chased away that of the galaxy. In the vision, a man stood looking over the shoulder of a woman. No, not a woman. It was this woman. In her arms, she cradled a small baby with a red tuft of hair that matched the color of the man's. Tony was shocked to hear sound this time. In the mental image, the woman was singing a song that Tony did not recognize. The music seemed to start and end inside his brain. The room around them looked similar to the interior of the ship. Very minimalistic with glowing walls. The woman bent over and laid the baby on a piece of furniture that seemed to grow up out of the floor as she bent. Tony belatedly recognized it as a crib.

Suddenly, something new came through his connection with the machines.

Emotions!

Not his own, but those of the woman in the vision. Tony could sense her pride, her love for her family.

His heart swelled with it.

Tears welled in his eyes. However, these were neither linked to the external emotions nor buffered by the calming effect exuded by the viral machines. These were his own, born of an unbearable loss.

Tony's emotions must've leaked back across the link he had with the woman because she suddenly looked at him with shocked, widening eyes that filled with tears. The terrible knowledge revealed to her by that connection streamed across her face.

Her mouth worked silently for a moment. Finally, she said, "I am sorry. Did not know."

"Don't worry about it," Tony whispered. He turned his head to the side, trying to blink the moisture from his eyes. He wiped the sleeve of his free arm across his face.

His body relaxed as he stopped straining against the bindings. Tony now knew that this was truly a human or Argonian woman, knew she couldn't have faked those emotions.

He lowered his arm and looked at her. "I believe you."

She nodded and extended her arm toward him.

Tony felt the floor release him. He accepted the proffered hand. Now standing on the tilted floor, he looked around the interior of the ship but saw nothing new, no control panel, not even the webbing that had suspended the woman.

He turned to face her. She looked tense as if expecting him to bolt.

"I am Major Anthony Spinelli." He held out a hand. "But you can call me Tony."

After the briefest hesitation, the woman grasped his hand and nodded. "Tony. I am Strem Kaspars."

"Casper? Like the friendly ghost?"

"Ghost? What is ghost?" Then her eyes widened. She looked at her arms and then looked back at Tony with a confused expression. "Me no ghost. I am alive."

Tony smiled and shook his head. "Don't be so literal, Strem."

The woman began to protest, but then a new noise drowned out her words. Tony recognized it instantly.

"That's a P-51 Mustang! Like the plane I was flying."

The woman started toward the breach in the hull, but Tony reached out and stopped her.

He held up a finger. "No, wait."

All they needed was for some wet-behind-the-ears second lieutenant with a happy trigger finger to start taking pot-shots at them.

The plane roared as it flew directly overhead. The saucer's two occupants stood motionlessly inside as the Mustang circled two more times. Finally, the fighter plane departed the area.

The woman looked at Tony with urgency in her eyes. "Must make radio call."

He shook his head. "I'm still not sure that's a good idea. I think we should wait for my leaders to make that decision."

"No!" Strem said, shaking her head. "There are procedures that must be followed," she said in her improving English. While her accent remained, the inflections of her speech had settled down, no longer emphasizing the wrong words. Strem gestured to the ship around them. "Some of these technologies are too dangerous for you. I must contact my leader."

Tony looked at her and held up his hands. "Why don't you have power?"

"Ship broken. Power source disconnected."

Tony pointed to the glowing walls and ceiling. "Looks like you have electricity."

Strem shook her head. "Not enough for radio, and my main power source is in ... I think you would call it safe mode. Cannot use. Disconnected."

She waved her hand in a beckoning motion. "Come see."

The woman walked to the opening in the hull. Tony followed. They stepped outside and walked around to the left side of the ship. She crouched down and pointed under the belly.

"The power source is—"

Strem stopped mid-sentence. She suddenly became very animated as she searched the underside of the craft.

"No ... No!"

Tony peered underneath, trying to see what had disturbed the woman so much. "What?"

"Not here. Gone!"

"What is?"

"Power source!" the woman said with a panicked tone.

Tony nodded. "Okay. I don't think we'll be alone much longer. The military will be here soon. We can figure it out then."

Strem shook her head vigorously. "Human Argonians cannot have power source. Definitely too dangerous."

"What do you mean? What kind of engine is it?"

"Not an engine, power source. Negative-material."

Tony tilted his head. "Negative-material?"

Strem appeared to consider his words. After a moment, she held up one hand. "Positive-material." Then she held up the other hand.

"Negative-material." She touched her hands together and then threw them apart, making a loud sound that must've been the Argonian equivalent of *boom*. "Positive meet negative make big ... giant ... *enormous*! Explosion!"

"You're talking about antimatter," Tony said, nodding contemplatively. "I just read an article about that in *National Geographic*."

Strem did not seem to hear him. The woman had a far-off gaze.

Unbidden, a new image appeared in his virtual vision. Tony saw a nuclear explosion. Then he blinked and his mouth fell open as he noticed the scale of the mushroom cloud in the image.

He was looking at North America, not as it would look on a map, this looked as it would from space, he guessed. There were no borders, and the continent was upside down, but the shorelines of the Pacific, the Atlantic, and the Gulf outlined its familiar shape. However, a towering mushroom cloud now sat where New Mexico should have been. It appeared to cover an area the size of the entire state.

Assuming that Strem saw it as well, Tony pointed into the image. "Is this what will happen if the antimatter gets loose?"

She nodded somberly.

Suddenly, the vision evaporated as a squeaking racket shattered the morning calm.

The two of them ducked for cover behind the ship. Peering around the vessel, they looked toward the mesa where the saucer had first impacted. A cloud of sand rose above its flat-topped surface. A moment later, a truck emerged from the billowing dust and slid to a stop at the hill's steep edge. A man stepped from its cab. Tony could just make out his denim shirt and straw hat but not much else.

The man was not looking in their direction. It didn't look like he had noticed the ship yet. He appeared to be studying something on the ground.

Suddenly, Strem stood upright, a shocked look on her face.

Tony held up a hand. "Don't worry about him. He's not with the military. That's just a local rancher."

The man suddenly kicked at something. Whatever it was, it must have been heavy. It didn't move.

Strem shook her head. "We need to stop him."

"What? Why? He can't do anything."

The rancher kicked the object again.

Strem stepped out from behind the ship and started jogging toward the distant man.

Tony followed her. As he caught up with the woman, he said, "What the hell are you doing?"

She pointed ahead. "Antimatter unit." Seeing Tony's sudden hesitation, the woman shook her head. "Is safe, contained. But kicking not good."

A couple of minutes later, as they began to climb the steep side of the mesa, a new noise rose. This time the squeaks and rattles of multiple vehicles filled the air.

Strem paused and looked at Tony with wide eyes. "More ... trucks?"

He nodded. "More something."

A dust cloud drifted overhead, this one much larger than the previous. As the sound of tires on gravel and sand ceased, multiple doors opened and then slammed closed.

Tony and Strem crept up to the lip of the mesa. Then they froze as an Army Air Corps Jeep zipped up to the edge of the hill. At the last second, it turned parallel to the precipice and slid to a stop, spraying Tony and Strem with sand and gravel.

CHAPTER 5

Clinging to the top of the mesa's steep slope, Tony and Strem hazarded a peek above its rocky ledge. A glossy, spit-shined boot descended from the far side of the Jeep.

"Good morning, Mr. Brazel."

"It's about time you guys got here," said the rancher, apparently one Mr. Brazel.

"We came as soon as we could, sir. As you can see, we needed to gather our men and equipment."

Peering beneath the Jeep, Tony could only see the boots of the two men.

"What do you have there?" the officer asked. "I thought you said you had aircraft debris."

Tony recognized the military man's voice. That was Major Jesse A. Marcel, a Roswell Army Air Field intelligence officer.

Tony looked from Major Marcel's spit-shined boots and spotted several more vehicles. It appeared that an entire military convoy had arrived while he and Strem had traversed the lowlands between the hills. Several men had already exited the vehicles and were rummaging through the debris that littered the hilltop. Some were already collecting the foil and depositing it into trucks. It didn't look like anybody had spotted the crashed ship yet.

Tony considered revealing himself to the major. He felt silly hiding, especially from an officer who shared the same rank as he.

"Well," the rancher said. "Thought it was a crashed plane the first time I spotted the debris. Saw it from my truck. That's why I called you. But now ... Well, I'm not so sure."

"We do have a missing fighter," said Marcel. "Sent out a spotter plane this morning. The pilot called in a crazy report about seeing some kind of ship. Seen anything like that?"

Tony gnashed his teeth. This was ridiculous. Why in the hell was he still hiding? He placed both hands on the top of the ledge.

Suddenly, Strem's hand grasped his upper arm. She looked at him with wide eyes. Then her voice manifested in his head. "No, Tony! They will take me." She tilted her head toward the sphere. "And they will take the antimatter, too. I won't be able to stop them."

Tony shook his head. To her, he subvocalized, "You can show them, just like you showed me."

She shook her head vigorously. "No, they will not let me close enough to insert the machines."

"I can tell them."

"They will think you ... contaminated. Isolate you. Not believe you."

"Nope," said Mr. Brazel.

Tony and Strem both winced as the rancher kicked the black sphere again.

"Not sure what I got, really," he said. "This is the first thing that I found that doesn't look like torn foil. Looks more like a basketball. But it's hard." He tried and failed to nudge it with the heel of his boot. "And damned heavy, too."

Tony cringed again as Major Marcel also kicked the black sphere.

Unbidden, the image of the state-eradicating mushroom cloud blossomed in his mind's eye again.

Tony gave Strem a hard look. Still subvocalizing, he said, "Stop it! I get it. I'll hold off ... for now." He paused and then gestured to the collection of soldiers and vehicles scattered across the hilltop. "But I'm not sure how in the hell we're going to get out of this."

Major Marcel raised his voice. "I need a few men over here."

Still peering beneath the Jeep, Tony and Strem watched several pairs of boots jog up toward the two men and the sphere.

Tony gestured for Strem to follow him. Together, they scrambled over the precipice and crawled under the Jeep, the sound of the approaching men covering their noise.

Marcel spoke up again. "You men lift this up and put it in the back of that Deuce and a Half over there."

The major and the rancher backed away as several pairs of dusty boots shuffled into position, surrounding the black sphere. With a chorus of grunts, the men hoisted the antimatter chamber waist-high and began shuffling toward the indicated two-and-a-half-ton truck. At a hundred feet away, it was the nearest of three large trucks presently parked on the mesa's flat top.

Tony turned urgent eyes toward Strem. "We're running out of time," he whispered. "They've almost collected all of the debris."

The woman nodded and closed her eyes.

Suddenly a loud pop issued from behind them.

Tony jumped, as did every visible pair of boots. Then he winced as the circle of struggling men flinched, dropping the antimatter chamber. It landed with a cracking thud. One of the men screamed in pain and fell, clutching his foot.

"What the hell was ...?" Major Marcel's words died mid-sentence as the mesa's entire complement of boots turned to face west.

Tony looked over his shoulder. The sound had come from the direction of the saucer. Sure enough, he could now see smoke pouring from its breached hull.

He looked at Strem's now open eyes. "What happened?" he said, subvocalizing again.

"I give machines an order, tell them to ..." She paused.

Tony felt the viral machines query his mind.

Strem nodded. "I gave them self-destruct order. Causes noise and fumes ... smoke."

"Will that burn up the whole ship?"

She shook her head. "Only the floor. It is a deck formed by billions of tiny machines."

Marcel's boots stepped up to the mesa's western edge, behind the Jeep.

A shiver ran down Tony's spine as he realized that he'd been lying on an ocean of viral machines. That's how she'd pinned him to the floor.

"What the hell is that?" Major Marcel said.

The rancher's pointed-toe cowboy boots stepped up to stand next to the major. "I don't rightly know. Hadn't noticed that before."

"Holy shit," Marcel said in a long, low whisper, barely audible from beneath the Jeep. His voice rose again. Sounding excited now, he started rattling off orders. "Corporal Jones, you and the other drivers take the trucks back and drop off what you've collected so far. Get me a trailer. Not a small one. We'll need one of those tank haulers. Stop by the motor pool and get the crane as well." After a moment's consideration, he hurriedly added, "And roust up the base's infantry company. We're gonna need several men to police this area. I want to make sure we pick up every piece of debris." He snapped his fingers. "Oh, yeah! Stop by the public information office and tell Lieutenant Haut I want his ass here two hours ago."

The boots of the apparent Corporal Jones snapped together. Tony could envision the young man's salute, although he couldn't see anything above his knees.

"Yes, sir," the corporal said.

A ringing noise echoed across the top of the hill as the still grunting men deposited the black sphere into the back of the two-and-a-half-ton truck.

Tony and Strem cringed again as the antimatter chamber rolled across the metal bed and slammed into its forward wall with another loud thud.

Now trotting away, Corporal Jones shouted, "Secure that load. Let's roll."

A minute later, the big trucks roared to life. They drove side-by-side away from Tony and Strem, toward the far eastern edge of the hill. The three identical trucks were too far away for Tony to make out their numeric markings.

Major Marcel spoke up. "The rest of you, with me!"

In a cloud of dust and with a chorus of surprised shouts, the remaining military personnel and the rancher careened over the edge of the hill and started trotting toward the crashed ship.

As all three trucks disappeared over the eastern lip of the mesa, Tony waved for Strem to follow him. They clambered out from under the far side of the Jeep. A quick scan of the hilltop revealed that they were indeed alone.

Tony eased the Jeep's transmission into neutral and released its parking brake. Then he motioned for Strem to help him. Together, they pushed the military vehicle away from the hillside. When enough of the hill sat between them and the running men to block the sound, Tony fired up the Jeep and waved for Strem to jump in.

Tony's heart raced with adrenaline. He wasn't sure what he would do when he caught up with the truck, but having it out of sight already had him nervous as hell.

Apparently, Strem was feeling the same anxiety. She looked at Tony and pointed ahead. "Faster!"

Tony nodded, but the two of them were already bouncing around in the seats. It was all he could do to keep the vehicle under control as it jittered across the desert. An agonizing minute later, they crossed the eastern edge of the hill. Tony saw the three trucks just as they pulled onto a nearby road, now driving in single file. He had no idea which one contained the antimatter chamber.

A short time later, the Jeep's tires squealed as Tony guided it onto the same highway. The vehicle's small engine roared as he pushed it to its top speed. Over the next several minutes they slowly closed on the small convoy.

Strem pointed ahead. "Which one?"

Tony shook his head. "I don't know. It was too far away. I couldn't see its markings. We are almost at Roswell Army Air Field. We'll just follow them to their destination and figure it out there."

He pointed to Strem's name tag. "That's backward." When the woman gave him a confused look, Tony pointed at his own name tag. "Yours is a mirror image of mine. The letters are reversed. You need to change it."

Understanding dawned on the woman's face.

Tony pulled his eyes from the road just long enough to see the tag morph, the letters reversing to properly spell out Spinelli. Still amazed, he shook his head but smiled. "That's better, but you need to pick a different name."

"What name?"

Tony envisioned one. "Can you see what I'm picturing?"

Strem nodded, and her name tag suddenly changed to Smith.

"Jesus! That's so weird. How are you doing that?"

She gestured to her uniform. "All made from tiny machines. Millions of them in a ... network."

Another shiver ran down Tony's spine as he contemplated wearing millions of viral machines as clothing. Just thinking about it made his skin crawl and itch.

He looked at Strem's hair and realized that, uniform or not, she'd never get through the gate looking like that. Tony pointed at her head. "Your hair is too long, and ..." He paused, shifting uncomfortably. "We don't have female fighter pilots. There used to be a few. They ferried planes during the war, but not anymore." Tony paused. He felt his face redden. Finally, he nodded toward her chest. "Your breasts are too big."

Strem smiled at his discomfort. Then she nodded and closed her eyes.

Tony flinched as silvery goo suddenly streamed out of the collar of the woman's imitation flight suit. It flowed over her head and began to change shape and color. An instant later, it looked identical to one of the Army helmets that the soldiers had been wearing, hanging chinstrap and all. She tucked her hair under the helmet.

Then she looked down. Suddenly the chest of her leather jacket flattened. He saw a wave of discomfort cross her face as a held breath burst from her lips.

Strem looked at Tony and grinned sheepishly. "Machines constricting ... compressing ..." She paused, searching for the word.

Tony sensed the query. Before he could stop it, the wrong word slipped from his thoughts.

Strem tilted her head. "Boobs?" Then she nodded. "Yes, the machines compress my boobs."

Tony felt his face flush again. He shook his head. "Jeez ..."

Ahead of them, the three-vehicle convoy passed through the base's gate. The Jeep was still half a mile from the entrance when Tony saw each truck go in a different direction. He slowed the Jeep and then pulled it over to the shoulder.

"Strem, can you tell, I mean sense, which vehicle has the sphere?"

The woman looked frightened. She shook her head. "No, I cannot."

Tony pounded the steering wheel. "Shit, shit, *shit*! What the hell are we going to do?!"

"I told you, need power source for my radio."

"What? How is that going to help you find it?"

"It won't, but I can call someone who can."

Tony nodded and then said, "Your English is getting better."

Strem pointed to her head. "Tiny machines, always learning."

His eyes narrowed. "Who are you going to call?"

"Someone that can stop this." As she said it, the now familiar image of the statewide mushroom cloud popped into his mind's eye.

Tony nodded. "Okay, okay, I get it." The image evaporated. He pointed at the dash of the Jeep. "There you go, twelve volts right there."

Strem shook her head. "Need more power. Antimatter power."

"Well, that's a real catch twenty-two."

The woman looked at him with a confused expression. "Catch twenty-two?"

Tony shrugged. "A dilemma, a logical conundrum."

After a long hesitation, Strem nodded her understanding.

"How much power you talking about?"

"Enough to open hole in space."

"A hole in space?" Tony said.

Another unbidden vision began to form in his mind's eye, but Tony raised a hand. They didn't have time for her to explain every arcane technological detail. "Never mind. There's a power plant near town." He envisioned the small, coal-burning plant in a way that he was pretty sure Strem could see.

It must've worked because she shook her head. "No. We need something bigger, more powerful."

"Bigger, huh?" He leaned back in the Jeep's driver's seat and stared across the desert for a moment. Then he raised his eyebrows. "I think I know of a place." In his mind's eye, Tony envisioned the site's iconic image.

Suddenly, Strem nodded and smiled. "Yes, that should work."

CHAPTER 6

Tony looked at his passenger and smiled. "You're gonna tear a hole in my upholstery if you don't release your white-knuckled death grip."

Strem shook her head and pointed at the vehicle's metal dashboard and then at the open sky. "Why does your Studebacon, sorry, your Studebaker not have an enclosure? No restraints, no padding?"

The grin fell from Tony's lips. He looked forward and glared at the streaming pavement. He swallowed, trying to banish the lump that suddenly tried to form in his throat. Today's events had given him his first reprieve from these thoughts, the memory of loss.

Out of the corner of his eye, Tony saw Strem staring at him confusedly.

Finally, Tony said, "Detroit seems to think that seat belts are only for airplanes, not cars."

The image of the highway wavered. He wiped away the threatening tears with the sleeve of his shirt and glanced self-consciously at Strem.

Her knuckles had turned white again.

Tony looked forward, following the line of her frightened gaze.

Another vehicle had just crested a hill, approaching from the opposite direction on the narrow highway.

His breath hitched. The accident had happened on a road just like this one. The thought dredged up the memories. That dark night, he'd learned why they called it heartache. The pain in his chest had been real. When the state trooper had deposited his terrible news on Tony's front door stoop, the sudden ache had felt as if someone were trying to wrench his heart from his chest. In his mind's eye, Tony could still see the message written across the trooper's face. Even now, the memory of that look brought back the emotions as if he were living it all over again.

Strem jerked as if jolted by electricity. She turned a shocked face to him. "Oh Gods ... Tony ... I-I am so sorry."

Tony's tear-filled eyes flared angrily. "Stop that! Get the hell out of my head!"

Strem looked at him silently for a long moment. Finally, she said, "Sorry for complaining about your car. I did not know."

When Tony didn't respond, Strem turned and stared at the desolate terrain scrolling across the passenger window. She batted tears from her eyes. He felt guilty for snapping at her.

The Studebaker gently rocked, and Strem flinched as the other car shot past them, traveling in the opposite direction.

Hoping to change the subject, Tony gestured toward the terrain. "Are there deserts on your home world, on Argonia?"

Strem wiped her cheeks again and then nodded. "Parts of it, yes. I grew up in a region much like this."

Since they'd fled Roswell, the woman's English had continued to improve, although she still had a thick, Afrikaner-like accent.

Strem turned her sorrowful eyes toward him again. He saw more apologies forming on her lips, but then her eyes widened, and her head snapped forward as the car crested another hill. Ahead, the road fell away precipitously, beginning a zigzagging course toward their now visible destination.

Happy for the distraction, Tony smiled and pointed at it. "There she is, Hoover Dam."

Strem looked at him for a long, silent moment. Then she nodded. "Okay, how are we going to get in?"

Tony held up the brochure he'd grabbed at the last service station. "According to this thing, the last tour starts at five PM." He looked at his wristwatch. "That leaves us fifteen minutes."

~

An hour later, Tony and Strem stood in the center of Hoover Dam's massive generator room. A giggling little boy pointed at Strem's ill-fitting khaki pants. "Hey, lady. Expecting a flood?"

She glanced toward the generator room's back wall with a confused look. Hoover Dam formed that end of the large room. She tilted her head and looked back to the boy. "No. Your dam is structurally sound. I don't think it will fail."

The boy rolled his eyes and then looked as if he was ready to say something else, but Tony waved at him dismissively. "Scram, kid."

The little boy laughed and ran back to the tour group.

Their guide raised an arm. "Now, if you'll follow me, folks, I'll show you the dam inner workings." The man smiled at his overused play on words.

Tony rolled his eyes and looked at Strem.

She suddenly coughed and winced.

Tony placed a hand on her elbow. "Are you okay?"

An odd look crossed Strem's face, but then she nodded.

They wore matching his-and-her Hawaiian shirts and khaki pants, clothes that Tony had pulled from his closet. Strem was taller than his wife had been, but the sight of those clothes and their associated memories still tore at his heart. Not wanting to start down that path again, he shifted his focus to the tan canvas backpack that hung from Strem's shoulder. He tugged it and pointed to a side door.

She nodded and then coughed again. Seeing Tony's concern, Strem said, "I am fine, but we are running out of time."

Tony returned the nod. For all he knew, the military might be hot on their heels, and he had no idea what they might be doing with the antimatter chamber.

He guided her to the back of the group. When the rest of the tourist passed through the large double doors at the back of the facility, Tony and Strem darted into the side room.

In its dark interior, Tony whispered, "Let's hold in here for a few minutes, make sure they don't come back for us."

"Okay," Strem said and then covered her mouth as she stifled another apparently painful cough.

After giving her a concerned glance, Tony looked around nervously. "Tell me again. Why couldn't we just tie into the power lines outside?"

Strem shook her head. "Those wires are too thin. We need to tap directly into the source."

"Well, I don't know if you noticed, but this place has armed guards. This could end badly."

She cocked an eyebrow. "Yes, it could."

Her tone told Tony that she wasn't talking about the guards or anything in the state of Nevada. Well, her tone and the state-sized mushroom cloud that the tiny machines suddenly pumped into his mind's eye.

Tony frowned. "Not helping."

A moment later, they peered from the small room and scanned the cavernous facility. A few technicians were working on one of the farthest generators, but their backs were turned to the two stowaways.

During the tour, Tony had seen a couple of armed guards roaming the room, but he couldn't see either of them at the moment.

He held a palm toward Strem. "Wait here." Then Tony pointed to the corner behind the nearest generator. "I'll go first."

Strem nodded. "Be careful."

Tony scanned the facility again and then returned the nod.

Feeling exposed, he slid through the door and scrambled across the open space, wincing at every sound emitted by his rubber-soled boat shoes. Finally, he darted behind the designated machine.

No one shouted. No alarms rang out.

After peering around the corner and seeing the technicians still working on the far generator, Tony waved for Strem to cross.

She scurried to his hidden corner.

Again, no alarms raised.

Without hesitation, Strem stepped up to the top of the massive hydroelectric turbine. The backpack hanging from her shoulders suddenly lost its shape and flowed from the woman's torso.

Tony shook his head. He'd seen the liquid movement of the viral machines several times now, but it still amazed him.

Like thickened mercury, the material flowed off of Strem and onto the side of the large generator.

The structure was the tip of a mechanical iceberg. The portion of the generator that protruded above the room's concrete floor was the size of Tony's apartment back in New Mexico. However, its bowels extended deep into the ground where they were attached to a turbine turned by the tremendous power of the lake's escaping depths.

Now the tiny machines flowed into a new shape on the upper portion of the massive generator. It looked like someone had added a new, futuristic device to it. Two silvery snakes streamed from the new machine and disappeared through a vent hole, winding their way deeper into the generator.

During their drive through Arizona, Tony had learned that the tiny machines were actually microscopic robots constructed at the atomic level. He couldn't imagine the technology required to manipulate individual atoms, but Strem had assured him that even Earth-based technology would master the basic physics in the next few decades, although creating computers and robots at that level likely lay far in our future.

Apparently, the microscopic robots could link their tiny computer minds into vast, powerful networks. Using their collected computing power, they could perform incredible feats. The network of virus-sized computers could intuit the need of their client and organize their collected mass into lattice formations to create larger and even macro-scale structures. They could take on shapes like the backpack or even the crib that had grown from the floor in Strem's nursery in the vision she'd used to convince Tony of her sincerity. According to her, they could even transmit light. A small sheet made from a few million robots could make something that would look like a paper-thin, flexible television screen.

Now the tiny machines had a much more complex feat to perform.

Strem closed her eyes momentarily, and the pitch of the generator's whine rose an octave as if its workload had doubled.

She looked at him and nodded. "It is working."

Tony watched wide-eyed as a small vortex suddenly formed about a foot above the new machine. The miniature cyclone sat superimposed over the backdrop of bars that covered one of the facility's upper windows. Viewed through the spinning construct, the parallel crossing lines of the iron grid skewed into a spiral, as if seen through swirling water. Tony leaned left and saw that the bars were still intact. They hadn't skewed. It wasn't the actual bars twisting, just the image of them as it passed through the vortex.

He pointed. "I thought you said it was too small to see?"

Strem had told him that the Argonians could affect real-time galactic-wide communications by creating a hole in folded space—whatever the hell that was. Apparently, they couldn't open a hole large enough to permit physical passage. Nothing with a wavelength longer than a gamma ray could fit through the subatomic-sized aperture.

That revelation had led Tony to ask how they traveled so quickly across the galaxy if they couldn't use "folded space." Strem had said they simply compressed space-time ahead of their ships and stretched it out behind. They called it parallel-space—another concept far outside of Tony's ability to grasp.

"That's not the hole, just the field effect," Strem said. Then she held a palm toward him and gazed intently into the swirling shape.

Then Tony glimpsed movement in his peripheral vision. Leaning to peek around the generator, he saw one of the armed guards heading their way.

"Strem," he whispered. "We are about to have company."

She didn't respond, only closed her eyes.

Suddenly, the vortex vanished, and the generator's whine returned to normal. The device formed by the virus-sized machines dissolved, losing its shape. The silvery material flowed down the side of the generator and started to cross the floor toward her.

"Strem!" Tony whispered urgently.

Suddenly, the mass split in half, and the closer portion flowed over his boat shoes and sped up his legs.

Tony felt panic trying to take him. Then he heard Strem's voice in his head.

"Don't move. Don't talk."

The mercurial material flowed up his chest. Then, to Tony's horror, it covered his face as well!

"Don't move," Strem silently urged.

The guard rounded the generator and stopped, looking directly at the two of them!

No. Not at them, through them.

The surprise Tony had expected to see on the man's face didn't manifest.

After a long moment, the guard shook his head and then walked away.

Tony's mouth fell open. He looked toward Strem. "Jeez," he whispered. "That was—" He stopped mid-sentence and started looking around. "Where'd you go?"

Suddenly, a portion of the back wall moved.

Tony blinked several times as his eyes struggled to find the right focal length. That part of the wall seemed too close, making his eyes cross uncomfortably.

Then a light cough came from right in front of him. A human-shaped portion of the background shook in unison with the spasm. Then the displayed image of the back wall's bricks drained from the top of Strem's head. Her face contorted as she stifled another apparently painful cough.

Tony saw the machines were flowing off of his body as well.

After they had covered the two of them, the fluorescing microrobots must have displayed an image of the background, camouflaging his and Strem's bodies perfectly, as long as they didn't move.

When the machines drained from Strem's hand, she covered her mouth to stifle another cough. It came away splattered with blood. The red effluence stained her teeth and lips as well.

The mercurial mass finished flowing from the two of them and rejoined, reassuming its backpack shape.

Tony stepped up to her.

"Strem? What's wrong?"

She pulled her gaze from her blood-covered palm and looked at him. "The machines are losing the battle."

"Wh-what?"

"When my ship crashed, the impact almost killed me. The machines have held me together since then, but now my body is failing faster than they can repair it."

"I don't understand."

"I'm dying, Tony."

He shook his head. "No, no, no. You can't die." He tugged her elbow. "Let's get you to a hospital."

Strem shook her head. "No! No time. They are coming."

"Who is coming?"

"My leader, Admiral Tekamah. You have to tell—" Another cough cut off her words. "You have to communicate with him."

Tony started to protest, but Strem turned from him and started walking toward the exit. He made a quick scan to make sure no one else had come to investigate. Then he followed.

A few minutes later, the pair reached the top of the dam. They had needed the micro-machine camouflage one more time along the way. Now they walked down the highway that ran across the top span of the mountain of concrete that held the Colorado River at bay, looking like a pair of drunks as they stumbled down its curved road. Several times, Strem nearly collapsed.

Finally, they arrived at Tony's Studebaker. Blood now flowed freely from Strem's nose and ears, scarlet tears even streaking her cheeks.

Tony had no idea what to do.

"This is my fault," he croaked hoarsely. "If you hadn't tried to save me in that damned storm, none of this would've happened."

Strem looked at him with sad eyes. "No, Tony. I'm—"

A gurgling wet cough cut off her words. Then the woman's knees buckled as they walked around the back of the car. Tony gently lowered her to a seated position.

Strem leaned against the Studebaker's chrome bumper. Now wheezing, she said, "Listen to me, Tony. You need to talk to my leader, Admiral Tekamah. Help him communicate with your people."

"You want me to be a ... liaison?"

Strem looked confused for a moment. Tony sensed the machines translating the word. Then comprehension dawned in her bloodshot eyes, and she nodded. "Yes, liaison. You need to get my body to Tekamah and then help him understand."

"Your body?!" Tony said, almost shouting the question. "Let's get you to a hospital. We're not far from Las Vegas. There'll be one there!"

"Told you. No time. Besides. Don't worry. It's only a body." She paused and tapped her temple. "My memories are safe in here."

"What are you talking about? If you die, that's it. There's no coming back, Strem."

The Argonian smiled weakly and shook her head. She patted Tony's cheek. "Be the liaison. Get me to Tekamah. He'll know what to do."

"How? How do I get in touch with—?"

Before Tony could finish the question, Strem's head lolled. A wet breath rattled from her lips, and then she breathed no more.

"No, no. Oh God, no!"

CHAPTER 7

"This is so wrong," Tony said with a grunt as he pushed the rest of her body into the small trunk of his yellow Studebaker. "I'm sorry, Strem."

Peaked eyebrows worried deep furrows into his forehead. Beneath them, watery eyes gazed sorrowfully down on Strem's tarpaulin-wrapped body. The sheet had been too small to completely encase the woman, but so much blood had begun to stream from her, he thought that if he didn't wrap at least her head and torso, the body would leave a red trail behind the car.

Tony shook his head. "Forgive me, Lord." A lifelong Catholic, he crossed himself and then slammed down the trunk lid just as Strem's free arm tumbled out. The cracking sound generated by the impact made his stomach spasm, but empty, it had no contents to disgorge. Tony just dry heaved as he pushed the arm back in. Finally, the trunk snicked closed.

Physically and emotionally drained, Tony sat on his heels, head hung down.

"What ya got there, son?"

Tony's head popped up. In the weak light cast by one of the

parking lot's lamps, he saw the reflection of an Arizona state trooper on the chrome bumper. A smudge of blood darkened the image of the man. Tony placed his hand on the smeared gore and used the bumper to push himself upright. Judging by the relaxed posture in his reflected image, the man hadn't seen the body. Otherwise, Tony doubted the trooper would be standing with his arms crossed. More likely, the man would have a gun pointed at the back of Tony's head.

Standing fully upright, Tony wiped his wet hand on the side of his Hawaiian shirt, trusting the faint light and the shirt's loud colors to camouflage the blood stain. He turned and gave the man what he hoped was a disarming smile.

"Just finished changing a flat, officer." Tony made a show of brushing off his hands. He found they were still damp.

The trooper gestured to Tony's mid-section. "Did you pack the wheel bearing while you had it off? Looks like you got grease all over yourself."

"What?" Tony looked down and was shocked to see patches of blood covered his khakis as well as his arms. Fortunately, the flat light trickling from the parking lot's few lamps rendered them as black smudges.

The trooper chuckled and then pointed at the Studebaker. "It'd be a shame to dirty up the upholstery of that fine car. Is that the Commander Regal?"

"Uh, yessir." Tony nodded. "The Regal Deluxe." Glad for the distraction, he looked around, seeking something to use to wipe away the worst of the blood before a passing car could shine the light of truth, revealing the nature of the stains that covered him.

Before stashing Strem's body, Tony had moved the overnight bag and the "backpack" into the Studebaker's back seat. He pointed to the former. "I have a rag."

He started to extend a hand toward the overnight bag, but then something he could only describe as a mental nudge caused him to reach for the backpack instead. As his hand neared the pack, its yellow canvas flap slid open, revealing a large rag, just like the one Tony had envisioned.

He plucked the cloth from the backpack and began to rub it over his arms and pants. In his palm, the sheet of tiny machines felt as flexible as a rag but colder, heavier, too. It passed effortlessly over his skin but seemed to drag a little as he wiped it across the dark stains on his tan pants. To Tony's amazement, the rag removed all of the blood, leaving clean skin and spotless khakis in their wake.

He saw the trooper pull a flashlight from where it had hung next to his still-holstered gun. Fortunately, he directed the beam into the Studebaker.

"Sure is a pretty car."

Tony nodded as he continued to wipe the blood from himself.

Suddenly, the officer's flashlight beam fell on Tony's pants.

The trooper froze. "What the hell?"

Tony stopped rubbing the wetness from his neck and looked up. The uniformed man was focused on Tony's pants. Fortunately, his hand still hadn't strayed to the butt of the gun on his hip.

"That's one helluva rag, son." He shook his head. "I'd have sworn those pants were ruined."

"It was just some road grime."

"If you say so." The trooper's light traveled up. Then he winced. "Ouch, looks like you scraped your knuckles."

Tony's eyes widened at the sight of the blood on the back of the hand that held the "rag." He moved the cloth to the other and wiped at it. "Yeah, the tire tool slipped."

Bright headlight beams suddenly swept through the parking lot.

Both men turned toward the source.

Tony's breath hitched, and his blood ran cold.

"They found me!"

The roar of the Military Police Jeep's engine drowned out his words. Then a chorus of other engines and sweeping fans of light beams, all from unseen sources, joined those of the Jeep. Both men took an involuntary backward step.

The trooper nudged his hat back. "What the hell? There were no convoy permits issued for tonight."

Three two-and-a-half-ton trucks—similar to those Tony and

Strem had followed from the crash site—crested the hill behind the Jeep. To Tony's relief, the line of westbound military vehicles followed the bend in the road, electing not to continue straight into the parking lot.

The trooper pointed back up the road. "What the hell is that?"

Multiple fingers of light shined from behind the rise of the highway, piercing the night sky. Then a row of six roof-mounted lights crested the hill. Beneath them, a giant truck cab and then several more sets of lights rose above the roadbed. The high-pitched whistle and the almost subsonic thrum of a supercharged Detroit Diesel engine shredded the night air.

Tony finally recognized the vehicle. It was an Army tank transporter. The massive tractor reached the bend of the road and turned left, following the rest of the convoy on its westerly course. The truck's low-slung trailer and its cargo passed into the dim light that fell from the parking lot.

Tony blinked and flinched, staring in open-mouthed amazement. Instead of a tank, the truck was hauling a large, wide load. A massive tarpaulin—similar to the one that currently nestled Strem's ruined body not five feet away—concealed the trailer's cargo, but its top had a dome shape. To anyone else, it probably looked like a tank of a different sort, one made for holding water or fuel. But Tony knew that profile. It was burned indelibly into his mind.

The crashed saucer.

Strem's ship!

The Arizona state trooper's indignation seemed to grow tenfold as he watched the military convoy cross Hoover Dam and continue onto the Nevada side, out of his jurisdiction.

"That's a goddamned wide load! They're definitely supposed to get a permit for that. There are fees! Even for Uncle Sam, dammit!"

As he watched the trailing Military Police Jeep crest the far hill and disappear, Tony was keen to follow.

"Well, officer. Guess it's time for me to head home."

The trooper shook his head one final time and then looked away from the illegal convoy. He shined the beam of his flashlight up and down Tony. "Well, at least you won't soil that pretty car."

"No, sir," Tony agreed as he stuffed the rag into the front pocket of his khakis.

The two men turned from where they'd watched the convoy and walked toward the Studebaker, the bright yellow spot of the flashlight's beam leading the way. It looked white when it fell upon the car's canary yellow trunk.

The trooper stopped mid-step. The beam of his flashlight locked onto the Studebaker's chrome bumper.

"Son, you mind telling me what the hell that is?"

A crimson rivulet flowed from the trunk. It had crossed the bumper and was pooling beneath the back-end of the car.

Tony tensed as he felt his options dwindling. He needed to follow that convoy, needed to get away from the trooper, but both prospects now seemed unlikely in the extreme.

"Uh," he stammered. Suddenly, the cloth in his pocket changed shape. Still in his hand, it felt as if it had taken on the familiar form of a pistol grip.

No! I'm not going to shoot this man, he sent to the machines in his head.

Stun him. Temporary, they replied in their wordless communication. Again, the thoughts came as the intentions of the terms, not the words themselves.

Tony saw the trooper's hand easing toward the butt of his service revolver, so he pulled the rag-turned-gun and pointed it at the man.

"I'm sorry for this, sir."

The trooper held up his hands. "Wait! I have a fam—"

Tony reluctantly squeezed the device's trigger.

With a loud snap, two wires launched from the silver pistol. Their ends appeared to burrow through the man's thin uniform shirt and embed themselves into his underlying skin.

The crackle of electricity chased away the sound of the snap. Then the trooper's legs gave out, and he collapsed, slumping into a twitching and groaning heap on the black surface of the parking lot.

A moment later, the wires retracted back into the "pistol."

An urgent, wordless message suddenly echoed through Tony's head.

Run! Go now!

CHAPTER 8

Tony watched the last of Las Vegas's city lights dwindle in the Studebaker's rear-view mirror. To either side of him, a bright moon rendered the desert in monochromatic shades of gray. A couple of miles ahead of the onrushing car, the military convoy and its alien cargo crested a rise in the highway and then descended out of sight.

The night birthed a sign on the right shoulder. Black letters on a white background announced:

Indian Springs 5 Miles

As he neared the top of the small rise, Tony glanced down at the map again. The military vehicles would likely hang a left at Tonopah and head to Reno or continue to San Francisco.

Tony looked up from the map as the Studebaker crested the rise in the road and instantly yanked his foot from the car's accelerator.

"Where'd they go?!"

The convoy was gone!

Ahead of his now coasting car, the small town of Indian Springs and its puddle of street lights filled the desert lowlands, crowding the right side of the northwest-bound highway.

As the yellow convertible sailed down Highway 95's long decline, Tony spotted the military vehicles. They had pulled into a service station.

He guided the car onto the shoulder and doused its lights.

Tony didn't dare pull into the station. The convoy had likely come from Roswell Army Air Field. The easily recognizable flowing lines of his yellow convertible would garner an unhealthy level of attention, especially considering his current AWOL status and the sensitive nature of both his and the convoy's cargo.

No, he'd just wait here.

Once the military vehicles returned to the highway, Tony would coast into the service station and top off his tank as well.

A few minutes later, the lights of the convoy flared into life. Tony watched intently as they poured from the station's gravel parking lot, launching a fresh cloud of dust that disappeared as soon as the night's light breeze carried it out of the range of the lot's feeble lighting.

To Tony's dismay, the line of vehicles turned away from the highway, heading north.

He tilted his head. "They're heading to Creech Air Base?"

That didn't make sense. Tony knew the area well. Since before the end of the war, he'd been flying training missions all over this region. The War Department had ordered Creech Army Air Field closed earlier this year. Since March of 1945 until just recently, they'd had nothing but a small housekeeping staff. Tony knew because he'd used the field as a refueling stop on numerous bombing and gunnery missions over Nevada Training Area Eighteen, but since January of this year, even that was no longer available.

The Studebaker reached the service station. Tony drove past it and guided the car into Indian Springs. The convoy had already passed through the small town and into Creech Air Base. Due to the bowl shape of the region's alluvial plain, he could easily see the convoy as it motored toward the airfield's entry gate.

Tony sat bolt upright. "They didn't stop!"

The line of vehicles had driven past Creech's gate without so much as slowing. Headlights and tail lights illuminated the cloud of dust kicked up as the convoy left the base's paved surface and started up a dirt road, headed north.

"Where in the hell are you going?"

Tony pictured the region from the air and suddenly knew.

Only one thing lay in that direction: Indian Springs Auxiliary Field Number 1, up on Groom Lake. There wasn't much there, just two runways on a dry lake bed with a couple of hangars on the side.

That was it! Had to be where they were headed. It was perfect. Far enough away from prying eyes. Hell, even commercial flights didn't venture over the region due to all of the high-altitude military training. And most of those Army Air Corps flights took place in Training Area Eighteen. Tony hadn't ventured into the airspace over Groom Lake, Training Area Fifty-One, in over a year.

Through narrowed eyes, Tony watched the last of the dust-clouded tail lights disappear around a small hill. His gaze shifted to the Studebaker's fuel gauge. In the convoy's direction of travel, there were no towns or service stations for another hundred miles, but he knew they'd be stopping long before that.

He nodded. "They'll keep."

Tony flipped a U-turn and headed back to the service station.

CHAPTER 9

Tony raised the binoculars to his eyes again. He squinted, glaring through their single serviceable tube, absently sweeping another bead of sweat from his forehead with the back of his right hand.

The sun had only been up for ten minutes, and Tony could already feel the temperature rising. Glistening heat waves made the most distant portions of the dry lake bed look as if water filled its arid expanse. The mountains beyond reflected off their shimmering waves.

Looking through the field glasses was only marginally better than his naked eye. Dust caked the edge of each lens, and scratches obscured much of its field of view. One of the tubes couldn't even focus. Tony didn't think the previous owner could see through that eye anyway. When he'd entered the gas station, the old man behind the counter had been using these to look at a jeans-clad Lucky Strike girl on the billboard across the highway. Tony didn't even want to think about what the old geezer had been doing before his arrival. The acquisition of the crumby binoculars had cost Tony twenty dollars. They probably weren't worth five cents.

He raised them up to eye level again. Peering through the good tube, he studied the hangar at the far side of the dry lake bed. The Military Police Jeeps had parked outside. However, the three two-and-a-half-ton trucks had disappeared inside the large, metal building.

Tony had arrived at this mountain pass just before sunrise. As he'd neared Groom Lake, he had doused the Studebaker's lights, slowing but not stopping until a well-lit guardhouse had slid into view. Fortunately, the two guards manning the checkpoint hadn't seen the car. He made a quick retreat and parked the Studebaker behind a nearby gully. Then Tony had wormed his way onto this perch. The small ledge overlooked the lake bed, but a rocky outcrop sat between him and the two men in the guard shack, screening him from view.

He leaned forward, peering around the ledge to see if they had noticed him.

"Is this Major Spinelli?"

Tony flinched and scampered backward. He rolled onto his back quickly, holding the binoculars up like an improbable shield.

No one stood above him!

He was still alone on his dusty perch.

"Where the hell did that come from?" he whispered.

"Major Spinelli. I am Admiral Tekamah."

Admiral Tekamah? Tony thought.

"Yes. Strem told you about me."

Tony looked around, desperate to find the source of the strangely accented voice but then felt foolish as he realized it was the damned micro-machines again.

"Where are you?" Tony subvocalized as he peered around the corner, making sure that his startled movements hadn't alerted the guards. Fortunately, they still looked bored as they stood chatting and smoking.

"We are parked above one of your oceans, just outside of your atmosphere. Do you still have Strem with you?"

Tony glanced back at the Studebaker and its macabre cargo. Then he nodded. "Yes, I do. But ... she didn't make it."

"I understand."

The man seemed rather nonchalant about the news. Maybe he hadn't registered Tony's true meaning.

"She's dead, Admiral!"

"I understand," Tekamah repeated flatly. It may have been a limitation of the communication medium, but the reply almost sounded uncaring. The admiral seemed disinterested in further information.

Tony shook his head but continued. "I think I've found the antimatter."

"You have," the disembodied voice said matter-of-factly.

"Wait. How do you know? And how are you communicating so well? It took Strem hours to speak this good."

"Her micro-machines, I believe you called them, transferred the language data to me during the connection when Strem warned me of your situation. As to your other question, I can see you, and my ship's sensors have located the antimatter pod. It is safe for now, in a building not far from you."

Tony nodded and peered through the usable tube of the binos. "I figured it must be in that hangar."

Then he heard the familiar thrumming propellers of a four-engine cargo plane. It sounded like a C-54 Skymaster.

"One of your airplanes approaches."

Tony nodded. "I hear it."

Then he saw light from the rising sun glint off of the surface of a silver cargo plane as it crested one of the mountains that ringed the eastern edge of Groom Lake's dry bed.

Tony raised the field glasses again. Then his eyes widened.

"Holy shit ..." he whispered. He tried to quell the next thought. Tony felt certain that he could trust this admiral, but he'd sworn an oath to protect and defend. And that man was—

No! Tony screamed inwardly at himself. *Don't even think it! Can't reveal his identity!*

The admiral's voice returned. "Who is Harry S. Truman?"

Tony's eyes closed. Then he shook his lowered head. "Shit!" His shoulders slumped, and he sighed. He knew the admiral was here to help, so he may as well know who else was here.

Finally, Tony nodded. "That's President Truman. Uh ... the leader of the United States, my country or nation."

"Your leader? You know this just by seeing the airplane?"

Tony nodded. "Definitely."

That was the C-118 not a C-54, same manufacturer and similar design but longer and sleeker than the older model. Douglas Aircraft had just begun delivering the first militarized DC-6s to the Army Air Corps that month, but this one had an eagle's face and beak painted across its nose and blue feathers on its tail. The military had only ordered one with that paint scheme, the President's, and this had to be one of its first flights.

The confirmation given by Tekamah coupled with this development removed any doubt: the saucer and its wreckage were in that hangar.

The long, silver plane had dropped low over the lake. After reaching the western edge of the dry bed, it reversed course in a slow, graceful turn. Now headed toward the two hangars, the pilot eased the plane down. As it landed, billowing clouds of dust boiled up from all three of its large tires. The C-118 coasted to a stop between the parked Jeeps and the hangar. The easterly wind carried the tan dust clouds clear.

Through the one good lens of the binoculars, Tony watched a big silver door just aft of the wings swing open. A tall set of stairs rolled out of the hangar and up to the opening.

A man in a tweed suit emerged, returned a salute from the men below, and then descended. While he was too far away for Tony to see his face, the curved-brim Stetson atop the man's head clinched it.

"That is United States President Harry S. Truman, Admiral."

The men waiting at the bottom of the stairs, likely Army Air Corps generals, lowered their salutes and led the President into the hangar. Then the trio disappeared, swallowed by its dark interior.

From his perch, Tony couldn't discern anything inside the large, metal building. Other than a flickering light from an unseen source, the hangar's interior was completely black against its bright exterior and adjacent lake bed. He was about to report as much when the admiral spoke up, his words suddenly animated and urgent.

"We have a problem! The internal temperature of the antimatter chamber is rising!"

Tony remembered the vision of a New Mexico-sized mushroom cloud expanding above the continent.

"Oh shit," he whispered. He raised the binoculars again. Light still flickered in the hangar's dark interior. His eyes widened with sudden comprehension.

"They're trying to open it with a cutting torch!"

"Go now, Major Spinelli! I am on my way, but I fear I may not arrive in time. Whatever they are doing, you must disrupt them!"

Tony leaped to his feet and sprinted back to his car. He'd closed the roof of the convertible before driving up the dusty road. He hopped behind the wheel in the car's already warming interior and fired up the engine. A moment later, he was barreling up the dirt road.

When Tony rounded the corner, the two Military Policemen guarding the gate turned from the sight of the President's plane. The taller of the two men threw down his cigarette and held up a hand for Tony to stop. The wooden gate arm sat between two cliff walls where the road passed through a narrow ravine, so going around it wasn't an option.

Tony floored the accelerator, gesturing wildly for the man to get out of the way.

The Military Policeman didn't move!

Laying on the horn, Tony shouted, "Get the hell out of the way!"

He was about to lift his foot from the accelerator when the man finally dove for cover.

Tony winced as the Studebaker slammed through the wood plank that served as the gate, but then the admiral's voice returned.

"Hurry, Major! The chamber's internal temperature is reaching critical levels!"

Suddenly, a hole appeared in his windshield. Then it sounded as if his car had backfired. Tony looked over his shoulder and saw white light shining through a matching hole in the convertible's black ragtop.

"They're shooting at me!"

"That is the least of your troubles, Major. Don't stop!"

Through the car's small back glass, Tony saw both MPs, weapons drawn, aiming at him. He ducked down as another beam of light shone through a fresh hole. Then he heard the report of the gun followed by several more.

As he crossed onto the dry lake bed, Tony shifted the car into overdrive and mashed the accelerator to the floor. He began swerving the car to throw off their aim.

The gunshots stopped. Tony looked back to see the men scrambling into their Jeep.

The admiral's insistent voice returned. "Hurry, Major! You must disrupt them before it's too late!"

Tony shook his head. Two miles of flat sand lay between him and the hangar. His speed had topped out at seventy miles per hour. Good thing he'd opted for the overdrive. Without it, the car would've done well to top fifty. He lay on the horn, hoping the sound would reach the hangar and pull the men inside away from their work in time.

In his side view mirror, Tony saw the MP Jeep emerge from the rooster tail of dust kicked up by his speeding Studebaker. He was surprised to see that they were gaining on him. The military four-by-four must have been modified for speed.

Ahead, Tony saw movement at the base of the President's airplane. Now less than a mile away, he saw two men start walking toward him with arms raised, motioning for him to turn back.

Tony flinched as his left mirror shattered. The reports of more gunfire came from behind him. He heard the pop of a bullet striking the trunk and gnashed his teeth as he pictured it punching through Strem's poor body.

Peering over the edge of the metal dash, Tony rocked the steering wheel left and right. Then the men ahead of his swerving, speeding car stopped waving and pulled out their sidearms and began to fire as well.

Tony ducked just as two new holes appeared in the windshield, raining glass shards down on him.

"Stop shooting at me! I'm trying to save you, dammit!" The Studebaker's blaring horn and the staccato reports of multiple gunshots drowned out his words.

Then Tony heard the sound of popping metal again, this time from the front of the car. He ventured a peek above the dash. Steam boiled up from under the car's hood, washing across the windshield. The engine began to stutter, and the horn fell silent.

"Shit!" Tony tried to press the accelerator harder, but it was already mashed to the floorboard. The engine continued to hitch, further slowing the Studebaker.

Suddenly, the shots fell silent both fore and aft. Tony hazarded a glance above the dashboard. He swerved, narrowly avoiding running over the two Secret Service men. They stood transfixed, looking up, slack-jawed, weapons hanging limply at their sides. In a fractured remnant of his side view mirror, Tony saw the Jeep slowing, its occupants looking up with open-mouthed amazement as well.

Ahead, light still flickered in the portion of the hangar visible through its open doors. Finally, the last of the Studebaker's inertia carried it through them, into the dark interior of the large, metal building.

Strem's ship sat in the hangar's back corner. In front of it, flaring yellow light silhouetted several men. The rushing roar of an industrial cutting torch drowned out even the Studebaker's roughly idling engine. Then the car died with a final backfire. The ring of goggle-clad men flinched at the loud report.

The cutting torch flickered and then died, plunging the hangar's interior and its occupants into a dark, silent void. The arc of men turned as one toward the new arrival. As they did, Tony glimpsed the black sphere between them. The top surface of the antimatter chamber glowed cherry red.

Still sitting in his steaming, bullet-ridden Studebaker, Tony held a hand out of the driver's door window. "You need to stop doing that!"

The men pulled off their dark goggles, but instead of looking at Tony, they turned and stared outside.

Tony exited the steaming car and saw President Truman step out of the center of the group. He, too, stared past Tony. "What in tarnation happened?"

Now that his ears had adjusted, Tony heard a new sound filling the air: an almost inaudible deep hum that set his teeth on edge. He could feel it vibrating his bones.

Before Tony could turn to see what the President was looking at, the man who'd been operating the industrial cutter jumped back. "What the hell?!" he shouted, stumbling backward.

The still glowing black sphere had lurched into the air. It hovered over the man's head for a moment and then rocketed toward Tony. He flinched, but the black orb passed over his head and disappeared behind him.

Tony turned to look outside. "What—?"

His words died.

The sandy dry lake bed looked dark as night, but the surrounding mountains still sat bathed in the sun's brilliance.

The bone-rattling hum faded and died. Then Admiral Tekamah's strangely accented, disembodied voice returned. "Excellent work, Major. The antimatter containment chamber has stabilized. The temperatures are dropping below critical."

Tony walked through the hangar door with the group of men. Emerging into the darkened desert, he looked up and stopped mid-step.

A curving, dark surface blotted out the entire sky.

Tony felt his pulse race at the sight of something so large silently hovering only a couple of hundred feet above his head. His eyes frantically scanned the smooth, black surface, looking for a point of reference.

The mountains to his left and right still sat in sunlight, but the shadow of the thing extended to the edge of the dry lake bed. Miles wide, the silently hovering monstrosity appeared to be as large as Groom Lake.

An odd pattern traced jagged lines along the black, curved surface of the ship's belly. After a moment, Tony realized it was an inverted reflection of the mountains that ringed Groom Lake. However, just as he'd seen on the crashed saucer, the reversed colors and the black hole sun reflected on the skin made it look like a city-sized photo negative.

Suddenly, a portion of that skin directly overhead vanished, revealing a rectangular hole in the bottom of the ship.

Then something emerged from the opening.

All of the men took an involuntary backward step.

Like Superman coming in for a landing, a man—minus the cape—slowly descended feet first as if suspended by invisible strings.

President Truman spoke up. "Put those away, idiots!"

Tony blinked and looked over to see the Secret Service men raising their pistols. He extended an arm and opened his mouth to yell at them, but then the weapons snapped from their hands as if yanked out by a giant rubber band. In an instant they passed the descending man, heading in the opposite direction. Tony soon lost sight of the guns as their dark surfaces became indiscernible from that of the ship.

The lowering man wore a flamboyant uniform that would have looked right at home on a Buck Rogers set. A moment later, he touched down light as a feather directly in front of Tony and dipped his head a degree. "Major Spinelli," he said with an accent similar to Strem's. "It is a pleasure to finally meet you."

Tony stood open-mouthed, unsure of what to say. He could feel the eyes of the surrounding men on him—including those of the President of the United States.

The strangely dressed man held out his hand and nodded toward it. "I believe this is your customary greeting. I am Admiral Tekamah."

Tony hesitantly accepted the proffered hand and shook it. "P-Pleased to meet you, sir."

The President and his Secret Service men, as well as the generals to his side, exchanged confused glances as they cycled between looking at Tony and the admiral and then up at the belly of the hovering monstrosity.

The President appeared about to speak when the admiral turned to him and offered his hand.

"Hello, United States President Harry S. Truman."

The President hesitated. The two Secret Service men moved to stand between them, but then Truman shoved them aside and stepped forward. He took the admiral's hand, shaking it vigorously. When he spoke, his voice had its familiar nasal Midwestern accent. "I can't tell you how happy I am to hear that's not a Russian accent, Admiral."

CHAPTER 10

"That's one helluva collection, Admiral," President Truman said.

The two men stood side-by-side in front of the long, curving surface that formed the back of the admiral's office. Several weapons adorned the wall, everything from small arms with vaguely familiar designs to larger, alien devices.

Tony would have been lucky to correctly identify the business end of most of the weapons. Positioned behind the pair of leaders, he stood next to the two generals that had welcomed the President and nearly overseen the destruction of a goodly portion of the ole USA.

Truman pointed to one of the displayed weapons. "That one looks very familiar."

Tekamah nodded. "It is one of my favorites. Ancient: several tens of thousands of your years." He paused and gave the President a meaningful look. "It was constructed by our ancestors."

Tony blinked and did a double take. The weapon appeared to be only a few years old, and with a couple of exceptions, it looked like something you could buy today on Earth.

The President nodded contemplatively. "I have one very similar."

Tekamah returned the nod and pointed to Truman's side. "Yes. I believe it's right there."

President Truman grinned. "Yep, you got me. I carry it often. Was surprised you let me in here with it, but I have no doubt you could easily disable it if I tried to do something foolish."

Tekamah gave him a knowing smile and dipped his head.

Truman gestured to the pistol on the wall and opened his blazer, showing the admiral his sidearm. "Do you mind?"

"Please," Tekamah said.

The President reached in and pulled a silver revolver from a hidden shoulder holster. Raising it in a non-threatening manner, he positioned the pistol muzzle-to-muzzle opposite the ancient Argonian revolver. The similarities in size and layout were remarkable.

Truman grinned and said, "This one is tens of thousands of years newer. It is an original Eighteen Seventy-Three model—the first year Colt made the Single Action Army revolver. That makes it about ... oh, seventy-four years old." He paused, raising the Colt a shade and then smiling wryly. "One whole year older than me."

Tekamah nodded appreciably. Then he gestured to the collection of weapons. "I keep these as a reminder of our violent beginnings, so that I remember our base ..." He frowned. "Our base nature."

President Truman—the first and only man ever to order a nuclear attack—nodded thoughtfully. Then he turned and offered Tekamah his antique Colt revolver. "Please accept this pistol as a gift, Admiral."

Tekamah looked uncomfortable for a moment, but then he smiled and took the offered revolver. He stepped up to the display and made a show of positioning it muzzle-to-muzzle opposite the Argonian one.

Tony saw the other men do a double take when the wall changed shape to support the new item.

The admiral stepped back. He turned and gave a curt nod to the President. "Thank you, President Harry S. Truman."

Truman smiled broadly and stuck out his hand. "Call me Harry."

Tekamah nodded and shook it. Then he gave the President a crooked grin. "Okay, Harry. You can call me Admiral."

Truman blinked, and his smile faded a notch.

After an uncomfortable silence, the President released the man's hand and stepped back. A hard, serious expression took over his features. "Alright, Admiral, what do you want from us?" He pointed to Tony. "Thanks to Major Spinelli, I do understand why you came here in the first place, but why have you invited us onto your ship and into your office? What do you intend?"

The admiral nodded. "I shall tell you." He gestured to the room's occupants and then to the smooth expanse of open floor. "Gentlemen, please have a seat."

The generals and the President exchanged confused glances. Then they stepped back as sections of the deck suddenly raised, flowing into the shape of chairs. Tony had seen this in the vision of Strem's home. It looked like a time-lapsed film of a melting ice sculpture run in reverse and greatly accelerated.

Two chairs manifested facing Tekamah's dark, wood-grained desk. An additional two seats formed left and right of the pair but farther back.

Truman stepped up to one of the center two seats. The ranking general stepped up to stand next to him.

The admiral shook his head. "No. This is for Major Spinelli."

Tony felt his face redden as everyone turned to look at him. He shook his head and stepped back, gesturing toward the seat. "No, thank you, sir—"

Tekamah held up a hand, cutting him off. He hoisted an eyebrow. "This is not a negotiation, Major." The admiral held out both hands. "Everyone, please sit." He regarded Tony with the eyebrow again and pointed for him to sit next to the President.

Tony stepped up to the indicated seat and cast an apologetic glance at the generals.

As everyone sat, Tekamah pointed at Tony. "My ... liaison, Major Spinelli, has already told you that we are of the same people. I believe that humans, as you call yourself, are descendants of a lost Argonian colony."

Truman tilted his head. "That makes no sense. How do you misplace an entire colony?"

The admiral spent the next several minutes briefing the President on the history of the Argonian people and their development, how they began to spread across the galaxy tens of thousands of years ago, not long after the making of the ancient revolver that now rested across from the Colt.

Near the end of the briefing, a room-spanning model of the Milky Way galaxy popped into existence over their heads. At first, Tony thought it was another trick of the micro-machines in his brain, but then he saw the other men staring up at it with open-mouthed wonder. He reached overhead and probed the glowing dust of stars. Unlike the virtual images, the light of these stars illuminated his hand. However, they didn't react to his touch. The modeled points of light appeared to pass right through his fingers.

As he finished his briefing, Tekamah extinguished the large rendering of the galaxy and looked at Truman with raised eyebrows. "Your thoughts, Harry?"

The President nodded ponderously. Then a smile crept across his face. "So you're saying that humans, excuse me, Argonians rule the galaxy?"

The admiral suddenly looked as if he'd tasted something sour. He shook his head. "Not rule. Administer. Yes, I believe that is the appropriate word."

"And you're saying there are other intelligent species out there?" President Truman said, pointing up.

The admiral nodded. "Yes, thousands of them."

"They all get along? They're all peaceable?"

Tekamah considered the question for a long moment. Finally, he shook his head somberly. "Not all could be labeled peaceable, but things have been ... peaceful for quite a long time."

Before the President could comment, the admiral continued. "It is unfortunate that we found you at your present level of development, both economic and cultural. Had we discovered you sooner, we could have reassimilated you more easily. As it is, I'm afraid we'll have to use the standard ..." He paused, appearing to search for the word.

Admiral Tekamah reached out to Tony via their connection, sending him the impression of the word he sought.

"Integration?" Tony said, not completely sure that had been correct.

Tekamah nodded. "Yes, the standard *integration* program."

Tony blinked, shocked by the underlying meaning conveyed by Tekamah's impression of the word.

President Truman tilted his head. "Integration program? Integrating what?"

Tekamah smiled. "Earth, humanity into the galactic government."

After a moment's hesitation, the President began to smile again as he appeared to consider the potential benefits for the United States.

Apparently seeing the same thing in the man's face, Tekamah shook his head. "No, Harry. This will not benefit the United States, not any more than it will all others."

Truman's smile faded a bit, but he nodded.

Tony knew that once the President understood the admiral's full meaning, he wouldn't be smiling at all.

EPILOGUE

At Tekamah's instructions, Tony followed a series of flowing lights up a long corridor. The interior of the massive ship looked like something right out of a European Gothic cathedral.

Ahead, the stream of gold light that ran along the floor turned and disappeared through a tall doorway. Bronze-colored fluted casing framed an opening that had a pointed arch at its peak. Tony reached the bend and stepped through. Mouth agape, he walked into the cavernous room beyond.

It looked as if he had stepped into an arena-sized terrarium.

Now standing in its middle, Tony slowly turned, scanning the room's interior. Rocky outcroppings protruded from every corner of the terrarium as well as its walls, floor, and ceiling. Plants of varying colors and textures adorned each. He even saw small animals scurrying amongst them, moving too fast for him to identify shape or form.

Turning from the doorway and its tall, pointed arch, Tony flinched and stepped back. "Holy shit! You scared the hell—"

He stopped mid-sentence. Blinking, Tony stared open-mouthed at the person who had somehow snuck in as he'd surveyed the room.

"Strem?"

The woman smiled and nodded.

"Strem!" Tony shouted and stepped up to throw his arms around her, but they passed right through the woman. His momentum carried him forward, and then he passed through her entire body, too.

Tony stumbled but remained on his feet. When he turned back to Strem, he realized that this was another projection, similar to the one that had modeled the Milky Way in Admiral Tekamah's office.

"You're not real," Tony said, suddenly dejected.

This was like rubbing salt in the wound, showing him the life he'd failed to save.

He started to walk out, but then the apparition raised an arm.

"Tony! Wait!"

He stopped mid-step and then slowly turned toward her.

"Strem?"

She nodded again.

He shook his head. "How can this be?"

Strem tapped her temple as she had in the Hoover Dam parking lot. "I told you, it's all up here."

"What? What does that mean? You're not here. This is just a simulation of some sort."

"No, this is me. Thanks to you, I'm whole again."

Tony waved a hand through her body. "You don't seem so whole to me."

She smiled and tapped her temple again. "I'm whole in here."

"In where?"

Her head tilted as she considered her words. Then Strem nodded. "You would call it a computer, but it is much more. All deployed or traveling Argonians reside in both their bodies and in the computer. It's a parallel existence maintained in real time by communications that pass through a hole in folded space."

"But your ship lost its communications link when it lost the antimatter chamber."

Strem nodded. "Yes, so I was disconnected from my computer-based half. Now that you have returned my body and the memories it contained—"

"You're whole again," Tony finished for her.

"Yes, my stream of consciousness is again one, and I'm home now in Argonia."

Suddenly, a man holding a baby manifested out of thin air, standing next to Strem. He nodded to Tony. "Thank you," he said in an accent even thicker than Strem's. Then he nodded again and disappeared.

Tony blinked and then looked at Strem. "They are in there with you?"

"Only until I get my new body."

Tony's head spun with the idea of it. He stared at the floor. A million questions stormed through him, but only one mattered. What about his own wife and daughter? He looked up to see Strem shaking her head, a profoundly sad look on her face.

"No, Tony. We can't bring them back."

His head lowered, eyes returning to the floor.

"But you did save me. You saved me for my husband and for my baby."

Tony shook his head. "No, you had a copy running in the computer. I didn't save you."

He looked up and saw Strem's head shaking again.

"You made me whole. There are ... complications when there is a break in the continuity of one's consciousness. It leaves the computer-based version feeling like a mere copy." She shivered, and her eyes drifted from him. Finally, she looked at him and smiled. "Thank you, Major Anthony Spinelli. You truly did save me."

Tony stared at her for a long moment. Then he felt something loosen inside him like an unrealized knot suddenly easing. Not all the way, not even half, but he thought this ... this might be bearable.

"I think ... I think you saved me, Strem."

She didn't respond, only gave him her Mona Lisa smile.

Finally, Strem said, "Interesting and challenging times ahead for you and your people."

Tony returned the nod. "Yes, yes there are."

"Do you think your leaders will adjust?"

Tony rubbed the back of his neck and shook his head. "I don't know. President Truman was none too happy about Tekamah's conditions." He frowned and then shrugged. "Time will tell."

Strem nodded. "Unfortunately, time is an asset of which your people will have ... perhaps ... too much."

Tony nodded again. "Perhaps, but I'll take today." He smiled hopefully. "It's as good a day as any."

<<<<>>>>

Thank you for reading First Contact!

Dear Reader,

I hope you enjoyed *First Contact*. Thanks for riding along with me on this journey.

I appreciate your feedback. Actually, you are the reason I write. While I work on my next novel, I'd love to hear from you. Tell me what you liked, what you loved, even what you hated. You can email me at dean@deanmcole.com and visit me on the web at www.deanm-cole.com.

Finally, I need to ask a favor. If you're so inclined, I'd truly appreciate a review of *First Contact*. In this day of e-marketing, you have the power to make or break a book. Please post a review for *First Contact* to its page on your favorite book retailer's website.

Thank you so much for reading *First Contact: A Sector 64 Prequel Novella* and for being my copilot on this adventure. Don't forget to follow me on your favorite site by clicking the appropriate links on the About the Author page.

Fly safe!

Dean M. Cole

Sector 64: Sneak Peek

The *Sector 64* Timeline

1947 - *First Contact* a *Sector 64* Prequel Novella

Today - *Ambush* - Book One of the *Sector 64* Duology

Tomorrow - *Retribution* - Book Two of the *Sector 64* Duology

Seventy years after the events of *First Contact,* most of humanity is completely unaware of the coming changes. We live and die believing we are alone. In 2017, Air Force fighter pilots Jake Giard and Sandra Fitzpatrick discover the decades-old secret project to integrate Earth into a galactic government, but then the plot renders our world a disposable pawn. An interstellar war spills onto our shores, plunging the planet into an otherworldly post-apocalyptic hell. Can Jake and Sandy save humanity from extinction? If you like action-packed, page-turning novels, then you'll love the electrifying action in this apocalyptic thriller.

SECTOR 64: AMBUSH SNEAK PEEK

Captain Sandra Fitzpatrick's steady rhythmic breathing, a technique born through years of cardio training, belied the horror gripping her soul. The teddy bear, oh God, the teddy bear. An image she couldn't shake, the vision would haunt her for the rest of her days.

Earlier, while jogging toward the distant terminal building, Sandy came across a still idling airport transfer bus. Hoping to use it to expedite the crossing, she peered into its closed glass doors. In spite of the eastern glow of the coming sunrise, she couldn't discern details through its dirty windows. However, the bus looked empty.

Jamming her fingers into the rubber gap between the panels, Sandy tried to pry the split glass doors apart. After a fruitless, half-minute struggle, she finally noticed a backlit, recessed emergency-release button left of the door. Activating it, Sandy heard a short blast of compressed air. She jumped as the doors popped two inches out of their opening and then parted, each sliding in opposite directions.

"Hello?"

No reply rose above the bus's droning diesel engine.

She took a tentative step into the opening. "Is anybody in here?"

Standing half in the doorway, Sandy screamed as two strong hands, squeezing from both sides, grasped her shoulders. Another blast of compressed air burped from under the bus, and the door trying to close on her retracted.

"Shit!" Sandy kicked the right panel of the retreating glass door and shook her head. Keep it together, Captain Fitzpatrick. She stepped all the way into the bus, and its doors slid closed. Air-conditioner blower noise replaced the engine's. Getting over her skittishness, she stepped into the driver's compartment. In the dawn's wan light, the seat looked empty. Groping in the darkness, Sandy worked her way closer. A few awkward seconds later, she finally dropped into it.

Something was wrong with the seat. It felt like someone had left a towel or cloth on it. Running her fingers across the material's loose, rippled surface, Sandy froze, remembering what she saw while peering down into the empty F-18's cockpit. An uncomfortable hard object dug into her right thigh. Wide-eyed in the dark, she leaned left and pulled it out from under her leg. Breathlessly holding the object up, she studied its angular silhouette against the deep turquoise hue of the early morning sky. A round ball on one end and a long rod on the other, it felt metallic. With her opposite hand, she blindly searched the instrument panel for a light switch. A huge windshield wiper arm sparked to life, its dry, rubber blade chattering against the dirty glass. Another switch later, the bus's cabin lit up like an exam room. Sandy blinked and squinted as the sudden blast of light burned her dark adapted eyes.

Finally able to see, she squinted at the device in her hand. Struggling not to scream, Sandy dropped the artificial hip. Jumping to her feet, she looked down to see a bus driver's uniform strewn across the compartment. While the driver's shirt was on the floor, the pants, belt still buckled, lay in the seat. She saw several shiny objects littering the interior of the pants. Bending, she looked closer. In a sudden epiphany, she recognized the parts as titanium screws.

What the hell could do that? She looked from the strewn articles, to the screws, and finally to the artificial hip where it had landed next to her right foot. Why isn't there any blood?

Backing away in shocked dismay, Sandy stumbled. Regaining her footing in the bus's central corridor, she looked aft and froze. Visible in the cabin's stark, white light, emptied articles of clothing littered the entire bus.

A glint of light drew her attention to one of the front left seats. A teddy bear's half-open, glass-bead eyes peered from under a vacated toddler's outfit. On the narrow bench, a little girl's tiny white and yellow dress sat between piled clothes of an apparent mother and father. Worn in anticipation of an early morning departure to some exciting destination, the tiny girl's yellow ribbons and pink bows now lay strewn about her emptied clothes.

Sandy had a mental image of the parents casting horrified glances at the monstrosity hovering overhead while they tried to calm their frightened little girl. But in Sandy's vision, she and Jake were the anxious couple. The child between them was the little girl with golden locks that she'd often imagined would grace their future. Unconsciously, her hand drifted to the point where the baby bump would soon show.

As a tear threatened to breach the levee of her lower eyelid, Sandy extended a trembling hand toward the stuffed animal. After a short hesitation, she caressed its furry belly.

The teddy bear's lifeless, doll-like eyes snapped wide open. "Are you my mommy?"

Find out why this happened and what happens next!

Get the Sector 64: Box Set Today!

SOLITUDE: SNEAK PEEK

Solitude: Book One of Dimension Space

The Martian meets *Gravity* when Earth's last man, Army Captain Vaughn Singleton, discovers that the last woman is stranded alone aboard the International Space Station. Commander Angela Brown could reverse the event that swept humanity from Earth's surface ... if only she could get there. If you like action-packed, page-turning novels, you'll love the electrifying action in this award-winning, apocalyptic thriller.

SOLITUDE: SNEAK PEEK

Angela looked down to see the familiar horseshoe shape of Hudson Bay glide beneath her white boots. She shifted her gaze to the south and spotted Canada's biggest annular lake. It ringed Manicouagan

Crater—one of Earth's largest asteroidal scars and easily visible from space.

"Uh, Commander Brown, if you're done sightseeing, I could use a hand here."

Angela smiled. Mindful of the ever-watchful eye of Mission Control, she resisted the urge to, playfully, hoist her middle finger. Instead, the commander gave him her cheesiest smile and said, "How may I be of assistance, Major?"

Major Peterson did a double take. He floated a few feet across from Angela. Behind the visor of his helmet, a crooked grin spread across his ebony face. "Really, Commander Brown? Assistance? What happened to, 'What can Brown do for you?'?"

Angela sighed and rolled her eyes. "Don't you start, too." Inside her helmet, her head shook side-to-side. "Crack one public joke, and it follows you around for the rest of your life."

"That'll learn ya," Bill Peterson said with a smile.

Angela ignored him and continued. "That was 2018. It's been two years. I mean, really?!"

Paying no heed to her, the major wrapped his gauntleted hand around a coffee cup-sized white cylinder. His body writhed as he struggled with the stubborn electrical connector.

The pair of astronauts floated near the left or port end of the International Space Station's 300-foot-long solar array truss. The structure supported all sixteen of the station's main solar panels. To Angela, the long edifice looked like the mutated body of a dragonfly with way too many wings.

"This thing doesn't want to budge," he said with a grunt. The man's entire body lurched as he tried to force the electrical connector to turn.

"Is that Charlie Eight One Niner?" Angela said.

After giving the connector's three-inch-thick barrel a final fruitless twist, he released it with a frustrated growl. "The one and only!"

The two spacesuited figures floated in the shadow of the station's outermost solar panel, but sunlight reflected off the truss, illuminating the major's face. He looked from the cylindrical connector and winked at her. "Got a can of WD-40?"

Angela smiled and held up a large set of white pliers. "Nope. But I do have the convincer."

She tilted the joystick grasped in her right hand. The bracket under her feet vibrated, and the robotic manipulator arm attached to the bottom of her boots moved the commander toward Major Bill Peterson.

A moment later she released the controller. Now they floated face-to-face: Angela standing on the end of the long manipulator arm, Bill clipped to the array's hard points, the offending power coupling between them. A metal label riveted to its side read:

C819

Angela grasped its outer ring with the convincer—a tool specifically designed for stubborn connectors. In the zero-G environment, she relied on the stability of Canadarm2, the manipulator arm strapped to her feet, to give her the leverage that she needed to apply a twisting force to the wrench.

The sticky connector finally broke free on her third attempt.

With a crackle of breaking squelch, a new voice blared from the radio speaker. "Great job, Commander."

"Why, thank you, Houston," Angela said. "While I have my tools out, is there anything else ... *I* can do for you?" She glared at Bill and silently mouthed, *Thanks, butt hole!*

In 2018, when UPS had brought back their old slogan, she'd asked a pesky reporter, "What can Brown do for you?" The S.O.B. had run with it. His editor had even made it the title of the front-page article. It had stuck, and now two years later, even she had almost uttered the damn thing!

"Actually, Commander Brown, there is something you can do for me."

Angela suddenly realized that the voice belonged to Randy McCree, the director of Mission Control.

"Oh … hello, Director. To what do we owe the pleasure?" Angela said, wincing inwardly. She resented the nervous feeling in her gut. The young physicist hadn't asked for this assignment, hadn't wanted it. In fact, Angela would've been happy if they'd left her to her experiments.

Ahead of the space station, Iceland appeared on the eastern horizon. Behind them, the inverted white triangle of Greenland's southern tip retreated, slowly sliding behind the curving line of the planet's western limb.

"Got something I'd like you to take a look at," McCree said.

Angela's head moved back and forth as she scanned the long solar array. Great! The woman had only been mission commander for a week, and on her first spacewalk, she'd already screwed up so badly that someone had summoned the director.

Apparently, NASA's ever-watchful eye was focused on her at that moment. Randy McCree chuckled. "It's nothing to do with your work. You'll need to look a little farther away to check this issue."

"Okay," Angela said, drawing out the word. "What do you have for us, Director?"

"Need you to take a look at Europe."

"Europe? Have you guys misplaced France … again?"

After a pregnant pause, the director's voice returned flat and humorless. "It seems we might have."

Commander Brown and Major Peterson exchanged confused glances as their smiles faded.

Randy McCree didn't wait for her to reply. "A few minutes ago, several data centers went quiet. Our hackers can't get anything from them, either."

Angela knew that by hackers he meant Information Technologies, or I.T. for short.

"Did they lose power?" Major Peterson said.

"No. There just isn't any new or active data coming through them. Since then, the problem has only worsened."

"Um, Houston, I'm not sure what we can see or do for you from here. I mean, Teddy is pretty good with computers. But—"

"All the servers are in Central Europe," Randy said, cutting her off. His voice had acquired a frazzled edge. "But there's more. We can't raise anyone on the phone either. And all of the region's news networks went silent, too. There's a satellite looking at the area." He paused as if searching for words. "But what we're seeing ... It doesn't make sense."

The cold blue waters of the North Atlantic scrolled beneath the ISS. Their current track across the planet would soon take them over Ireland, Britain, and indeed, France.

"I need human eyes on this thing," Randy McCree said.

Commander Brown knitted her eyebrows. "Thing? What are you seeing, sir?"

"Well, it almost looks like an aurora."

Angela and Bill exchanged concerned glances. Exceptional auroras usually signaled the arrival of particularly energetic solar discharges—something that could prove fatal to astronauts not within the metal walls of the space station.

"Is it a coronal mass ejection, sir?" Commander Brown said calmly, relieved that her concern hadn't crept into the words.

"No, no, no. We haven't had any CMEs in the last several days, and certainly, nothing pointing toward Earth. No, this is something else."

Angela started breathing again and opened a station-wide channel. "Teddy, I need you in the Cupola."

"What's up, Command-Oh?" the Russian crew member said, his mock SoCal surfer boy accent lilting each word.

Angela looked ahead. Beneath the aft end of the port or leftmost forward-pointing solar panel, she watched Ireland's rocky shoreline crest the blue horizon. Overhead and to her right, the long, articulated truss that connected all sixteen of the station's main solar arrays extended 150 feet to the structure's midway point. There it connected to the line of modules that formed the body of the ISS. Between her and the intersection, banks of solar arrays extended left and right like mirrored wings.

The woman looked forward again. As they continued eastward,

she glimpsed an upside-down reflection of Ireland on the bottom of the outermost solar panel.

Movement to her right front drew her eye. In the faceted windows of the Cupola, a blond mane drifted into view. Even from 200 feet, she could see it filling a significant portion of the station's observatory.

"Jesus, Teddy! I told you to tie that back," Angela said and then reopened the connection with Houston.

"Hey, man. Don't be hating on the 'fro."

The commander cleared her throat. "Um, Mission Specialist Theodore Petrovich, we're on with Director McCree."

Teddy donned a navy blue baseball cap that sported the circled red chevron of Roscosmos, the Russian Federal Space Agency. The hat reined in his blond mane. Inside the observatory, the man held up his palms in a what-gives gesture. His mock Valley intonation morphed back into his almost clichéd Russian accent and dropped an octave. "Da, Commander. I'm in position." After a brief pause, he added, "Good morning, Director McCree. What can *Brown* do for you?"

Angela shot him an angry look that went unnoticed by all but Major Peterson who chuckled lightly by her side.

"Telemetry shows that you are about to pass over Ireland," the director said. "There's an atmospheric anomaly we'd like you to take a look at. It's over England now and approaching their west coast. So you should—"

"No way!" Teddy interrupted, the return of his Russianized SoCal accent drawing out the words. After uttering a few others in his native tongue, he said, "What in the *hell* is that?!"

To Angela's right, Bill twitched. "Son of a ...!" he said with a tone of shocked awe. After casting an embarrassed glance toward the commander, he pointed east.

She looked forward, and her eyes widened.

A curtain of white light was rising above the horizon.

"Oh my God," Angela said in a whisper.

The commander could see why the director had compared it to an aurora. In the upper reaches of the atmosphere, its light faded to black in undulating feathery fingers.

Then the full height of the thing rolled into view, and the comparison collapsed. The colorful sheets of the aurora borealis usually ran in faint curving lines that never quite reached the planet's surface. However, this thing's light extended all the way from the edge of space down to the ground.

"That's no aurora," Bill said.

Angela nodded wordlessly, unable to speak. This was wrong, very wrong.

The curtain of white ... energy? ... appeared to run in a perfectly straight line left and right until it disappeared over the curve of the north and south horizons.

What the hell could create something like that? she wondered.

The director's voice snapped Angela from her reverie. "What are you seeing, Commander?"

"Houston, we've spotted the ... the anomaly." Breathlessly, she added, "It looks like a wall of light!" Her respiration rate had doubled. The astronaut swallowed, trying to rein it in. "But not like an aurora. The light reaches all the way to the surface. I-I can't see through it!"

The damn thing was high, too high!

"Houston, I'm not sure we'll clear it!" Bill Peterson said. "Looks like we're flying straight at it."

The ISS's ever-arcing orbital path sent them careening toward the white wall. Its upper reaches extended high above the planet. The opaque curtain concealed everything beyond it. It looked as if the space station was rushing toward the energetic rampart like a doomed moth on a collision course with a planet-sized windshield.

Angela's entire body tensed. Pain radiated from her clenched fists. Then the planet's eastern horizon slid into view over the energy curtain's upper reaches, and she relaxed a shade. If they could see the horizon beyond the anomaly, they must be above it. Right?

As their path carried them closer to the wave, Europe and then England and even the Isle of Man slid into view behind the wall. In the highest reaches of the ever-thinning atmosphere, the anomaly appeared to fade and then disappear completely. But the commander had no way to know if its effect—whatever that effect might be—extended above that point.

Angela's body began to tense again as the thought took root like a weed.

Inexorably, the ISS continued east, racing toward its date with the anomaly.

Looking down now, she watched the base of the wave move across the surface, advancing westward, moving in the opposite direction of the ISS. The wavefront raced across the Irish Sea. As the station passed over the Cliffs of Moher on Ireland's western shore, the curtain of light swallowed Dublin ahead to the east.

She held her breath as they sped toward the upper reaches of the anomaly.

"Here it comes!" Teddy shouted.

The commander crossed forearms in front of her helmet. To her right, Bill had the same involuntary response. "Oh God!" he yelled.

Head turned slightly, Angela watched through narrowed eyes as the wall rushed at them. North and south, its extremities appeared motionless, but the central section rushed at them with impossible speed, closing the gap in milliseconds!

Find out what happens next. Get Solitude: Book One of Dimension Space Today!

ABOUT THE AUTHOR

Author, world traveler, and combat pilot turned commercial helicopter pilot Dean M. Cole writes from locales as remote as Equatorial Guinea and as romantic as Paris's Champs-Elysées with his trusty sidekick and beautiful wife, Donna. A combat veteran, he flew Apache Attack Helicopters in the US Army's First Cavalry Division.

Follow Dean on BookBub

BookBub

For More Information:
https://www.deanmcole.com
dean@deanmcole.com

Made in the USA
Monee, IL
18 October 2026

66035041R00062